CIARAN'S BOND

HIGHLANDER FATE BOOK THREE

STELLA KNIGHT

PRONUNCIATION GUIDE

Ciaran - KEE-uran
Lachaid - LACH-ee
Gabhran - GAW-run
Donella - DON-ela
Eoin - YOE-in
Tavish - TAY-vish
Walrick - WAL-rik

CHAPTER 1

A chill crept through Isabelle as she maneuvered her rental car through the narrow cobblestoned streets of Larkin. The village, nestled in the Scottish Highlands, was the intended destination of her friend Fiona, who'd gone missing months ago.

Was this the last village you saw before you disappeared, Fiona? Isabelle wondered, tightening her grip on the steering wheel. This quaint village hardly seemed like a site for mysterious disappearances, but she'd recently learned of another missing woman—Kara Forrester, a journalist from New York. She'd vanished a few weeks ago after leaving her inn here in Larkin, the same inn Isabelle was heading to now.

Isabelle expelled a tense breath as she pulled

up to the inn, the only one in the village, a brick building that resembled a large cottage. She shut off the ignition and leaned back in her seat, her heart hammering in nervous anticipation.

Since arriving in Scotland a couple of days ago, Isabelle had searched nonstop for Fiona, retracing her friend's steps. She'd flown into Aberdeen, just as Fiona had weeks ago, before driving to Inverness. The innkeepers at the bed-and-breakfast where Fiona had stayed were as unhelpful as they'd been the first time Isabelle came searching. They'd told her the same story: the last time they'd seen Fiona, she'd left the bed-and-breakfast with her sketching materials, and she'd left alone.

After leaving Inverness, Isabelle had driven west, stopping at a few small towns and villages along the way, where she'd shown Fiona's photo to patrons at inns and pubs. But no one recognized her.

Isabelle looked down at her shoulder bag on the passenger seat. In it she'd stored a letter Fiona had sent her weeks ago, insisting she was fine and urging Isabelle to not look for her. But given that Fiona wrote the letter on ancient-looking parchment with no return address, Isabelle was suspicious. Disappearing the way she had was so out of character for the kind and thoughtful Fiona that Isabelle's worry had only increased. Since it was summer and the high school where she taught was out of session, Isabelle had taken the opportunity to resume her search.

And she'd let herself entertain something she'd previously dismissed. When Fiona first disappeared, Isabelle had spoken to an elderly bartender in Inverness who'd told her of a village, Tairseach, where it was rumored that people just . . . disappeared. Isabelle had dismissed this as superstition, but ever since receiving Fiona's mysterious letter, the story had tugged at her mind. She had tried to talk to the bartender again, only to learn that he'd recently passed away.

It'll do you no good to entertain superstitious rumors, Isabelle told herself. She needed to focus on facts to find her friend.

She climbed out of the car, stretching her aching limbs. She'd driven for hours and it had taken a toll on her legs. She turned, surveying the picturesque streets of Larkin. The tiny village was something right out of a postcard, with its winding cobblestone streets and vintage-style cottages and shops that lined them.

As she took it in, a rush of determination filled her. Maybe there were answers here. Answers she'd missed before.

Isabelle entered the bed-and-breakfast, where a petite middle-aged woman who introduced herself as Sophie greeted her.

"Here are your keys, dear," Sophie said, handing Isabelle a set of keys after checking her in. "Your room is the first door to the right down that corridor."

"Thanks," Isabelle said. She bit her lip as she

studied her. Sophie may have already answered questions about Fiona from the police, but it couldn't hurt to ask more. "May I ask you something? Have you seen this woman by any chance?"

Isabelle took out her phone, handing it to Sophie. On the screen was a photo of her and Fiona; it was the last photo they'd taken together outside of a dive bar in Chicago. Isabelle had taken her there to commiserate over Fiona's breakup with her fiancé, Derek. It was there that Isabelle had convinced Fiona to come to Scotland for her honeymoon—solo.

"I'm sorry, dear. I'm afraid I don't recognize her," Sophie said with an apologetic smile.

Isabelle's heart sank. But she swiped to another photo, this one of Kara Forrester, the other woman who'd gone missing from Larkin.

"Do you know anything about this woman's disappearance?" Isabelle asked, hoping she didn't sound too desperate. "She went missing from your inn a few weeks ago."

Sophie stiffened, her friendly smile vanishing. She looked at Isabelle with narrowed eyes.

"Are you with the press?" she demanded. "Because I already told the police everything I know."

"No," Isabelle said fervently. "I'm just looking for my friend. I—I thought maybe there was a link between their disappearances."

"I wouldn't know if there was," Sophie returned. "I'm sorry about your friend, truly. But I don't know anything. You'd have to go to the police."

Isabelle swallowed her disappointment, giving her a shaky nod. It would do no good to press Sophie for information she didn't have. She turned to head to her room.

"Wait."

Isabelle turned. Sophie's expression softened; she gestured for her to come back to the counter.

"I'm sorry. We've had nosy reporters and conspiracy theorists bother us ever since Miss Forrester went missing. I can tell you this—Kara only stayed here for a night before she went missing. Didn't say a word to anyone. A friend of hers, Jon, called and inquired about her after she disappeared. He might be able to tell you more. I can give you his contact info if you'd like."

"Thank you," Isabelle whispered, feeling a rush of something she hadn't experience since Fiona went missing. Hope.

When Isabelle settled into her room moments later, she leaned back against the door, looking down at the slip of paper where Sophie had written Jon's contact information. She could only pray that he knew something that could help her.

Tears stung her eyes as she thought of Fiona. She'd taken a liking to her as soon as she began working as an art teacher at the same high school where Isabelle taught English. They'd spent many lunch hours in the teacher's lounge commiserating over rowdy students, annoying fellow teachers, and their lousy pay. Their relationship soon blossomed from friendly coworkers to best friends as they got to know each other. Though they were different personality wise—Fiona was more shy and reserved, Isabelle bold and outgoing—there was much they had in common. They were passionate about the subjects they taught; Fiona loved art and was a skilled artist in her own right, Isabelle loved classic literature and tried to pass along that passion to her students. They both had little in the way of family—their parents had died long ago, though Isabelle had a brother Scott with whom she was close.

She and Fiona had become each other's family in a sense, and Scott cared for Fiona as a sister. He'd helped Isabelle with her search for Fiona when she first went missing and regularly contacted the police in Inverness for any updates on Isabelle's behalf.

Guilt pricked at her chest as she thought of Scott; he lived in Edinburgh, where he worked as a professor of classics at the University of Edinburgh. She owed him a phone call. She'd barely been in touch with him since arriving in Scotland; her search for Fiona had consumed most of her time. But she was heading to Edinburgh for an extended visit with him and his wife after her search. She hoped that Fiona would be at her side when she did.

She took out her phone, looking down at the photo of her smiling friend.

"Fiona," Isabelle whispered to her friend's photo. "Where the hell are you?"

~

"Wait—you got a letter too?" Jon asked in disbelief.

It was early the next morning, and Isabelle had arranged an online call with Jon to discuss Kara's disappearance.

Now, he stared at her from her laptop screen, his eyes wide with astonishment.

"Yes," Isabelle said, her heart picking up its pace.

"I received something similar from Kara," Jon said slowly. "It was a letter written on parchment. She wrote that she couldn't tell me where she was, but that she's happy where she is and to not look for her."

Isabelle leaned back in her chair, her mind reeling.

"That can't be a coincidence," she whispered.

"No," Jon agreed, "it can't. But—listen. It hurts she didn't tell me she was planning to leave for good and chooses not to stay in contact, but I believe her when she says she's safe."

"What do you mean?" Isabelle asked, her body tensing. "You don't want to find her?"

"I do, more than anything. But knowing Kara, she'd kick my ass for tracking her down against her wishes. I don't blame you for wanting to find your friend, and I'm not suggesting you shouldn't. But I'm going to leave Kara be."

Isabelle closed her eyes, gritting her teeth in frustration. She'd hoped Jon would join her in the search, especially given the similarities of their friend's disappearances.

"Well, I need to confirm with my own eyes that Fiona is safe," Isabelle said firmly. "Did Kara say anything to you? Anything . . . weird before she left? Anything that would indicate she didn't intend to come back?"

"Well," Jon said, after a long pause. "We met up for lunch before she flew to Scotland. And she talked about some weird stuff during our meal."

"Like what?"

"She asked me if I believed in . . . aliens. The supernatural. That there was something her late grandmother wanted her to do, but she wouldn't tell me what it was."

Isabelle went still, her mind immediately going to Tairseach.

"I basically told her to go for it, to do this mysterious thing her grandmother wanted," Jon continued, a look of guilt flickering across his face. "You have no idea how much I regret saying that now. It clearly influenced her decision to leave—forever. But from her letter, wherever she is . . . she's happy. Look, I wish I could be of more help, Isabelle."

Isabelle sighed, rubbing her temples. It seemed the more questions she asked, the more questions popped up, like a frustrating game of whack-amole. Kara asked Jon if he believed in the supernatural before she disappeared. Why? Did she know about Tairseach? Was Tairseach linked to something supernatural? Unease crawled through her as she thought of the rumored disappearances there.

"And . . . there's one more thing," Jon hedged.

"What?"

"Before I got Kara's letter, I did some digging on my own. Made some calls. One of my contacts told me of rumors about a place called Tairseach."

Isabelle froze, her heart leaping into her throat. Jon met her eyes, giving her a grim nod as he took in her expression.

"I take it you've heard of it."

"Yes," Isabelle said, licking her dry lips.

"Well, my contact told me there's one rumor that gets buried among all the tales of disappearances. A pretty big one."

"And what is that?"

Jon seemed reluctant to continue, leaning back in his chair and raking a hand through his hair.

"Jon," Isabelle said. "Please."

"This is crazy and I don't believe it for a second. But the rumor is . . . that it's not *where* these people are disappearing to," he said, holding her gaze. "It's *when*."

CHAPTER 2

1390
Aitharne Castle

Ciaran rested his head against the cold stone wall of the dungeon, closing his eyes. His cell reeked of dirt and piss, and the stench of rot hung in the air. He'd put many men in these dungeons over the years, but as laird of Aitharne Castle and chieftain of Clan Aitharne, he never thought he'd spend time in one.

He opened his eyes, watching as a rat scampered across the dirty cell floor. He focused on the rat's movements, trying to keep his mind blank, trying not to think of the crime he was imprisoned for. A crime he didn't commit.

Footsteps approached his cell, and Ciaran forced himself to his feet. He recognized the guard who approached—Angus, a young man whose family he'd helped during the last plague that swept over their region of the Highlands. Angus kept his eyes cast down to the floor, avoiding Ciaran's gaze.

"'Tis all right," Ciaran said gruffly. He could tell Angus didn't like having to hold his chieftain in the dungeons like a criminal. "Ye're just doing yer duty."

Angus gave him a jerky nod but kept his gaze on the floor.

"Yer brother and the nobles want tae see ye," Angus said, unlocking his cell door and stepping aside. He reluctantly took hold of Ciaran's arm and led him down the dank corridor that led out of the dungeons.

"Ye should ken, m'laird," Angus said, lowering his voice, though they were the only ones in the dungeons. Ciaran stiffened at the title Angus used, the title he'd been formally stripped of the day before. "Yer brother has evidence he means tae use against ye."

Icy dread coursed through him, but Ciaran kept his features stoic.

"I wouldnae expect no different," Ciaran muttered.

His brother Tavish was the one who'd had him arrested and imprisoned. He'd always know his brother hated him, but by the time he realized just how deep his brother's hatred ran, it was too late.

Ciaran tried to keep his calm as Angus led him up the stairs and down the corridor that led to the great hall. As they walked, the servants who milled past them avoided his eyes. Only days ago they'd answered to him as laird; now it was as if he were an imposter in his own castle. Anger spiraled through him, but he kept his expression neutral, even as Angus led him into the great hall.

Inside the hall sat a dozen of the clan nobles. The only true friend among them was a tall dark-haired and bearded man, Lachaid, who'd been his close friend since they were both bairns. Lachaid's dark eyes met his, a look of sorrow flashing across his face. Lachaid had tried in vain to prevent Ciaran's arrest and imprisonment, but as leader of the clan in Ciaran's stead, Tavish held the most power and had refused.

Another noble by the name of Ramsey also looked uncertain, barely meeting Ciaran's eyes. Ciaran had always liked Ramsey, who was an honorable man, but he too had to bow down to Tavish's orders when it came to Ciaran's arrest and imprisonment.

Tavish sat in the center of them all, glaring at Ciaran. Though they shared the same blood, he and Tavish looked nothing alike. While Ciaran had dark hair, hazel eyes, and their late father's towering height, Tavish was fair and stocky, with the blond hair and blue eyes of their late mother, passed down from her Norse ancestors.

Tavish's blue eyes flashed with hatred as Angus brought Ciaran before him and stepped aside.

"Ye have been accused of the murder of our dear brother Eoin, who was second in line to take

over for ye as chieftain in the event of yer death,"
Tavish said, his voice raised so that all the nobles in
the hall could hear.

Ciaran tried not to flinch at the mention of his
brother's name, the brother he had loved, the
brother who'd been savagely murdered. Grief, hot
and fierce, spread throughout his chest. *Ye didnae
deserve such a death, brother,* he thought. *I
should've been there tae protect ye.*

"We now have evidence that it was ye who
stabbed Eoin during an argument in yer chamber,"
Tavish continued, his eyes now gleaming with
triumph. He turned to look behind Ciaran. "Ye
may enter."

Ciaran tensed as two men entered the hall
behind him, approaching the long table. At the
sight of them, disbelief swirled through his veins.
One man was his trusted steward, Ian. The other
was a high-ranking noble he'd thought was his
friend, Walrick.

Neither of them met his eyes, keeping their
gazes trained on the nobles before them. Anger
replaced his grief, and he clenched his fists at his
side. What had his brother offered them for their
lies?

"These witnesses attest that they saw ye
murder Eoin," Tavish continued. "What say ye tae
their accusations?"

Ciaran turned to study Ian and Walrick, the
two liars. They returned his look with nothing but
coldness. He gritted his teeth. How could they

possess such dishonor? He wanted nothing more than to charge at them, to attack them for their lies.

But there was another emotion that filled him, one that surpassed his anger and even his grief.

Guilt. Guilt that he'd not seen the hatred Tavish held for him, hatred that propelled him to murder their brother and set Ciaran up for the deed. Guilt that he'd not protected the gentle and kindhearted Eoin from their brother's wrath. Ciaran's focus had been singled-minded, only on his power as chieftain and laird.

Before their father died, he'd asked Ciaran to watch out for his brothers. To protect them. And he'd failed in his most important duty.

"I am guilty," Ciaran said, his voice so low it was barely above a whisper.

But everyone in the hall heard him. The nobles' eyes widened in surprise. Even Tavish looked taken aback.

After a long moment of stunned silence, Lachaid shot to his feet.

"What the hell are ye doing, Ciaran?" he roared. "Ye didnae do this. Ye—"

"Lachaid, take your seat!" Tavish hissed. "Or I will have ye escorted from the hall."

"I am guilty," Ciaran repeated, his voice firmer now. "I'll take whatever punishment ye deem fit."

"No, Ciaran!" Lachaid shouted. "What are ye—"

"Guards, escort Lachaid from the hall," Tavish demanded.

Ciaran avoided Lachaid's panicked eyes as two guards escorted him from the hall. When Lachaid was gone, amid a hail of swears and curses, Tavish returned his focus to Ciaran.

"As yer guilt is confirmed, the punishment is death," Tavish said, a look of dark pleasure crossing his features. "Death by hanging. Yer sentence will be carried out in one day's time."

CHAPTER 3

Present Day
Romarty, Scotland

Isabelle parked her rental car in front of a small cottage and climbed out, surveying it with mild anxiety.

After dropping the bombshell about people disappearing "in time," Jon had directed her here, to the remote village of Romarty where a woman named Kensa lived. According to Jon, a local told him that she knew much about the mysterious disappearances.

She took a deep breath as she approached the front door, hoping this wasn't a fool's errand. It was early in the morning and she was still jet lagged; she'd not been able to sleep after getting off the phone with Jon.

Please work, she silently pleaded as she raised

her hand to knock on the front door. *Please know something.*

Before she could knock, the door swung open, and Isabelle blinked in surprise at the woman who greeted her. Jon had mentioned that Kensa was elderly, but the willowy dark-haired woman who studied her now couldn't be over thirty.

"Hi," Isabelle said, forcing a smile. "I'm Isabelle. I'm looking for a woman named Kensa. There's . . . something I need to ask her."

The woman looked at her for several long moments, recognition flaring in her dark eyes. Finally, she stepped back and gestured for her to enter.

"I'm Kensa. Please—come inside."

Isabelle obliged, surprised at her willingness to invite her in despite having no idea who she was or exactly why she was here. Isabelle took in the living room as she entered; it was cluttered and stuffed to the brim with ancient-looking books and old, tattered furniture.

She paused in front of a striking painting which hung on a side wall. A man in full medieval Highland regalia glowered at her from the portrait; he was short and balding with cold eyes. Even though it was only a portrait, a chill filled Isabelle at the sight of him.

"I collect old paintings," Kensa said, following her gaze. "Found this one at an antique sale in Inverness. That portrait is of Artair Brothaig. He was hung in 1392 for betraying several clans and profiting from their conflicts. He was not a nice man." She scowled at the portrait, before waving Isabelle to an overstuffed armchair in the corner. "I'll probably end up selling it back. Please, sit. Can I get you something? Tea? Water?"

"I'm fine," Isabelle said, looking away from the portrait as she perched on the edge of the chair. "I'm sorry to bother you, I'll make this quick. I came here because—"

"You want to know about the disappearances," Kensa said calmly, taking a seat opposite her.

Isabelle froze, eyeing Kensa with wary suspicion. How did she know?

"You're not the only person who's come here asking about the disappearances," Kensa said with a polite smile, answering the silent question in Isabelle's eyes.

Isabelle swallowed hard, reaching into her purse to take out her phone. She swiped to a photo of Fiona before handing it to her.

"My friend Fiona disappeared in this area a few months ago," Isabelle said. "She sent me a letter out of the blue insisting she was okay and to not look for her. But . . . it's not like her to do something like that. I'm still worried about her. "

Kensa barely glanced at the photo of Fiona before training her dark gaze on Isabelle for such a long moment that she felt unsettled.

"Then perhaps you should heed her request," Kensa said, handing Isabelle's phone back.

"Not until I know for sure that she's safe,"

Isabelle said, shaking her head. "If you know anything . . ."

She studied Kensa, hoping that she would give her something—anything. But Kensa's expression remained stoic.

"Sometimes people just disappear," Kensa murmured.

"No, they don't," Isabelle said, trying to keep her tone even. "Look, the person who sent me here, he said something about—something about people disappearing in time. And when I was first searching for her, someone told me about a place called Tairseach—a place where people disappear. I know it sounds crazy, but can it all be linked?"

"Ah, Tairseach," Kensa said, leaning forward in her chair, her gaze intent on Isabelle. "What else do you know about Tairseach?"

"Just that it means portal in Gaelic," Isabelle hedged. "But . . . I can't find it on a map, and my internet searches bring up nothing about the place."

"You won't find it on any map," Kensa said. "In this time, only people with the ability to travel can see it."

Isabelle's body went rigid. An icy chill spiraled around her heart, and her mouth went dry. Kensa's face remained serene, as if they were just having a casual chat about the weather.

"What are you talking about?" Isabelle breathed. "Travel? What do you mean—the ability to travel? Travel where?"

"You already know," Kensa said, giving her a cryptic smile. "You just don't know it yet."

Anger splintered her unease and Isabelle glared at her. She was fed up with the cryptic comments.

"Fiona is like a sister to me. If you know something that can help, I'm asking—" Isabelle took a deep breath, softening her tone. "I'm begging you. Please tell me."

Kensa remained silent, but Isabelle saw a trace of sympathy in her eyes.

"I don't know if you're ready for this," Kensa murmured. "It's rare that one of you find me. Usually I'm the one to find you."

"Please—enough with the vagueness. I don't know what you're talking about," Isabelle said, clenching her fists in her lap.

"Tairseach is indeed a portal," Kensa said, after a brief pause. "Long ago, during the time of the Celts, it was the home of druid settlers. It survived the Roman invasion, but one day the settlers just . . . disappeared. Those settlers are my ancestors."

"Okay," Isabelle said slowly, wondering what on earth this had to do with Fiona and the modern-day disappearances.

"Ever since then," Kensa continued, "certain people who come to Tairseach also disappear. But they don't just vanish. They fall through time."

Isabelle stared at Kensa, but she returned her gaze with absolute sincerity. Isabelle didn't know whether to laugh or cry. She closed her eyes, her shoulders sinking. Why had she entertained this crazy idea about people disappearing in time? She'd hoped Kensa would have actual information . . . some reasonable explanation as to where Fiona could have gone.

As someone who taught English for a living and loved books, Isabelle had a healthy imagination. But time travel was pushing things a little too far.

"Thank you for talking to me," Isabelle said, getting to her feet and forcing a smile. "I'll be on my way."

"Ah," Kensa said, shaking her head. "Since you came to me, I thought it was your time to . . ." she sighed, trailing off.

"My time to what?"

"Never mind. Go on your way. But I would trust your friend's letter. She's right where she belongs. It will do you no good to keep looking for her."

"Is there more you're not telling me?" Isabelle demanded. "Kensa . . . please."

"I've told you all you need to know. You're not ready. You choose not to listen."

Isabelle gritted her teeth. What if this was her last feasible chance of finding Fiona? She sat back down, forcing herself to calm down.

"You said the people who disappear at Tairseach . . . they fall through time," she said. She couldn't believe she was considering this, but she was desperate. "To what time? The Victorian era?

Roman times? And how do you know they're going through time?"

Kensa didn't answer, getting to her feet and walking to the door. She turned, giving Isabelle a sad smile.

"You can leave now, Isabelle."

"I'm willing to hear you out," Isabelle said, her desperation rising. "Can you tell me more?"

"You're not ready. Please leave."

The door abruptly flew open, and Isabelle gasped. Kensa hadn't made a move to open the door; it wasn't a windy day.

"Did—did you do that?" Isabelle whispered.

"You can leave my home now."

"Please," Isabelle said, getting to her feet. "I—I'm sorry for my skepticism earlier. I can accept there's something going on here that I can't yet understand. I *am* ready. Please . . . tell me more."

The door slowly drifted shut. Isabelle sucked in her breath, certain that Kensa had done it.

Kensa approached her, and Isabelle noticed something she'd missed before. There were now strands of gray in Kensa's hair and well-defined crow's feet around her eyes. While she'd looked thirty when Isabelle first came to her door, she now looked to be in her mid-forties. It was as if she'd aged fifteen years in the past fifteen minutes.

Isabelle's pulse fluttered wildly at the base of her throat as she realized that something was going on here. Something beyond her grasp . . . something otherworldly. She needed to set her skepticism aside.

"Very well," Kensa said. "But . . . it's better if I show you."

~

MOMENTS LATER, Isabelle and Kensa pulled over to the side of the road, stepping out of her rental car. They'd driven for only twenty minutes with Kensa riding shotgun. She'd directed Isabelle where to go but refused to tell her exactly where they were going.

As Isabelle got out of the car, she took in their destination. They'd arrived at an abandoned village filled with old crumbling buildings and the ruins of a castle on its outskirts. Isabelle surveyed it, tension filling her.

"Is this it?" Isabelle asked. "Tairseach?"

Kensa gazed at it with quiet reverence, and when she turned back to face her, Isabelle stifled a gasp. Kensa now looked to be in her late sixties; her hair was mostly gray, her face peppered with wrinkles. Isabelle took her in with dazed astonishment, shaking her head.

"What's happening?" Isabelle demanded. "Who are you?"

"Someone who wants to help," Kensa said simply. She reached up to touch her hair, expelling a sigh. "A side effect from my abilities, I'm afraid.

Come, Isabelle. This is what you were looking for. And yes, this is Tairseach."

Isabelle had a million questions, but forced herself to follow Kensa toward the ruins. She looked around at the medieval ghost town, suppressing a shudder. Was this where Fiona had disappeared? Kara Forrester? So many others?

"Is—is Fiona nearby?" Isabelle asked, a sudden unease gripping her.

Kensa didn't respond, continuing to make her way through the village until she reached the entrance to the castle. Isabelle followed, rubbing her arms for warmth as the light breeze around them suddenly picked up.

Kensa remained silent and still, gazing at the ruins of the castle. The wind gradually increased around them, whipping Isabelle's dark hair around, and she had to struggle to hold herself upright.

"What did you want me to see?!" Isabelle shouted over the force of the growing wind.

"I am a *stuireadh*." Kensa's voice was low, but Isabelle could hear her clearly, even over the roar of wind. "I help travelers get to where they need to be. Fiona didn't belong in this time."

A growing panic filled Isabelle, and she stumbled back. The wind was violent now, and she didn't know how much longer she could hold herself upright.

But the wind seemed to have no effect on Kensa at all. She gave Isabelle a look of utter calm.

She's crazy, Isabelle thought with horror, taking another faltering step back.

"What did you do?!" Isabelle shouted. "What did you do to Fiona?"

Kensa stepped toward her, gripping her arms. The smile she gave Isabelle wasn't cruel, or sinister. It was filled with genuine warmth.

"I sent her to where she truly belongs. You don't belong here either, Isabelle. It's time for you to go."

Kensa released her, and Isabelle lost control of her body. She screamed as the wind sucked her backward, lifting her off her feet, and her entire world went black.

CHAPTER 4

1390
Aitharne Castle

Ciaran sat huddled in the corner of his cell, his head buried in his hands, the memory of Tavish's hate-filled eyes filling his thoughts. He didn't regret confessing his guilt; it was true. While he'd not killed his brother by his own hand, he was guilty of not protecting him. He had failed his family. And for that he deserved his punishment.

"Ye damned fool."

He looked up. Lachaid stood by the door to his cell with a fierce scowl, clutching a sack at his side. Ciaran turned away from him, closing his eyes.

"Leave me be, Lachaid."

"If ye think I'm going tae let ye die and leave that murderous brother of yers in charge, ye're a fool."

Ciaran flinched at Lachaid's words. Though he

knew it was true, it pained him to think of Tavish as a murderer.

He turned back around, startled, at the clinking sound of a key unlocking the cell door. Lachaid swung open the door, pocketing the key.

"What are ye doing?" Ciaran demanded, stumbling to his feet. He braced himself for Angus to enter the cell at any moment, his sword drawn.

"I'm freeing ye," Lachaid said calmly, his thick eyebrows raised. "There's a horse and a bag of supplies waiting by the stables for ye, but we doonae have much time."

"No," Ciaran said swiftly. "I'll nae have ye hang on account of me."

"Yer guard Angus respects ye. He agreed tae look the other way, tae make it look like an outsider rescued ye. He kens ye didnae kill yer brother. Now if ye doonae leave this cell, I'll go tell the nobles I helped ye kill Eoin."

"Lachaid—"

"I speak the truth, Ciaran," Lachaid said, holding his gaze.

Ciaran studied his friend; he knew he was serious. As the son of a clan noble, Lachaid and Ciaran had grown up together; he was as close to him as any brother. Lachaid was fiercely loyal—and he never backed down from his word.

"Ye're a stubborn bastard," Ciaran muttered, though he gave him a grudging smile as he stepped out of the cell.

"As are ye," Lachaid said. He reached into his

sack, taking out a cloak. "Put this on. Keep yer head low."

Ciaran obliged, placing the cloak around his head and body, following Lachaid out of the dungeons. His heart thundered in his chest as they moved, expecting them to be caught at any moment, but he kept his gaze trained on the ground.

There were a few servants milling around the corridor as they emerged from the dungeons and into the castle, but no one looked their way. Ciaran held his breath until they were clear of the castle and had reached the rear of the stables. There, a horse was waiting for him, a sheathed sword and a bag of supplies slung over its flank.

"Get off of Aitharne lands," Lachaid said, as Ciaran took off his cloak and mounted the horse. "The nobles in power are mostly loyal tae yer brother, but there are a few on yer side. Try tae get messages tae me if ye can; I have some trusted messengers in the castle. I'm going tae do everything I can tae clear yer name while ye're gone. Doonae come back unless ye have an army riding with ye. Tavish is determined tae see ye hang."

Ciaran looked down at Lachaid, gripping the reins of the horse, a surge of emotion coursing through him. He wanted to thank his friend, to express his gratitude for standing by him when so many others had turned their backs, but no words came.

Lachaid knew him well and seemed to understand the words he couldn't say.

"Ye would do the same for me," Lachaid said gruffly, stepping back. "Now go—before the stable boys return."

Ciaran gave Lachaid a nod and turned to ride away from the castle, keeping his head ducked low. He resisted the urge to turn and look back at the turreted stone castle he'd called home his entire life. Instead, he kept his gaze trained on the road ahead.

Now that he'd escaped, he was officially an outlaw. Anger filled his chest, replacing the lingering guilt and despair he'd felt in his cell. He couldn't let Tavish get away with this. Eoin's death would not go unavenged. He would somehow clear his name and return to his castle to confront his brother and make him answer for what he'd done.

For the first time since his arrest, determination swelled within him. Ciaran kicked the sides of his horse, urging him to go faster. The sooner he found somewhere safe to shelter, the sooner he could make his plan to return.

Ciaran heeded Lachaid's advice, riding until he was clear of Aitharne lands. He soon entered the lands of a neighboring clan, Clan McCrosain. They were a friendly clan, allies to Clan Aitharne, but he still needed to stay out of sight. He didn't want them to bear the responsibility of harboring a fugitive.

Ciaran guided his horse into a forest that lined

the edge of the sprawling green moors, bringing him to a stop when they reached a clearing. He would have to make camp for the night until he determined where to go.

It had been some time since he'd spent the night outdoors; his hunting trips only took him away from the castle for a few hours at a time. He tied his horse to a tree, and a sense of calm settled over him as he set up camp. He'd spent the past few days in a cramped and dirty cell. It felt good to be outdoors, with its crisp air scented with damp earth and pine. A stream wound through the clearing, and the sound of its trickling water over rocks soothed him.

Lachaid had included provisions of food in his bag: bread and ale. He tore into the bread though it only partially satisfied the hunger that gnawed at his gut. He'd taken for granted the sumptuous feasts he had in the great hall on a daily basis, with the cooks preparing his favorite meals of sumptuous stews and roasted meats.

A sudden sadness filled him, not over the everyday comforts of the castle, but over the sense of isolation that settled over him. He loved Aitharne Castle, from its myriad of chambers and winding corridors, to the great hall where he'd enjoyed many a feast. The castle was filled to the brim with workers and servants who'd worked in the castle since before he was a bairn, many of whom were like family to him. Aitharne Castle had been in his family and clan for several generations.

But Tavish had desecrated his home with Eoin's murder.

He finished his bread, taking a swig of ale. It would do no good to mull over Tavish's treachery. He needed to focus on what he'd do next.

His thoughts wandered to a close friend of his: Gabhran. He lived not far from these lands with his wife and young daughter. Ciaran was reluctant to put him and his family at risk by hiding out with them, but Gabhran was his closest ally—and he had the resources and men to help him.

It was beginning to grow dark. Ciaran put aside thoughts of Gabhran as he used his cloak as a makeshift bed, lying down and allowing his heavy fatigue to claim him.

CIARAN AWOKE to the sound of a splash and a muffled curse. He was instantly on his feet, his hand flying to the hilt of his sword.

In the near distance, he heard more splashing. Gripping his sword, he moved out of the clearing, following the stream south.

He went still when he arrived at the source of the splashing, astonishment rendering him still.

A bonnie lass in breeches stood on the banks of the stream, as wet as a drowned rodent, her blue eyes wild with fear.

When the world righted itself around Isabelle, she found herself splashing about in a muddy stream. Startled, she looked around in astonishment. It looked like it was the middle of the night, and a thick patch of forest surrounded her. There was no sign of Kensa—or Tairseach—anywhere.

How was it night? It was barely afternoon when she'd come to Tairseach with Kensa.

Panic tightened her chest as she recalled Kensa's words, right before she released her arms. *You don't belong here either, Isabelle. It's time for you to go.*

Isabelle froze at the sound of someone's approach; twigs cracked and branches rustled. She stumbled out of the stream, shivering from the chill in the night air . . . and from fear.

Her heart leapt into her throat at the sight of a

tall and broad-shouldered man emerging from a thick patch of trees.

"Lass?" he asked. "Are ye all right?"

"Stay back!" Isabelle shouted, noticing the *sword* he carried at his side. She tried to remain calm, reassuring herself that at least it wasn't a gun.

He wore medieval clothing—a dark tunic and a kilt, both stained with dirt. She couldn't make out much of his face, given that it too was covered in grime, but his eyes were distinct; a hazel color that was an arresting mixture of brown, gray and green.

"I'm not going tae hurt ye, lass," he said, holding his hands up and tossing his sword aside. "Where's yer escort?"

"Escort?" Isabelle echoed. She could barely understand his thick Scottish brogue, and she was still preoccupied by his medieval clothing.

"Aye," he said, his brow furrowing with concern. "A lass shouldnae travel on her own at night without escort. Where's yer horse? Did harm come tae ye or yer escort?"

Isabelle just stared at him, her throat going dry. And all at once, the memory of Kensa's words slammed into her.

I help travelers get to where they need to be. Fiona didn't belong in this time.

They don't just vanish. They fall through time.

Only those with the ability to travel can see it.

Isabelle let out a sharp laugh, stumbling back from him. This was a prank. It had to be. An insane, ridiculous prank.

But the man was looking at her with nothing but utter sincerity. She drew a shaky breath.

"What—what year is it?"

"What year is it?" the man echoed, looking even more concerned now. "Lass, are ye certain ye—"

"Answer the question, please."

"'Tis the year 1390," the man said slowly.

Isabelle closed her eyes, gripping the side of the nearest tree to keep herself upright. It couldn't be 1390. That was impossible. There had to be a reasonable explanation.

"Can—can you point me to the nearest road?" she whispered.

"There's no roads nearby," the man said. "The closest ones ye'll find are muddy and unreliable, difficult tae make out in the dark. But even if ye could, 'tis not safe for ye tae travel on yer own. Is that why ye're dressed in those strange breeches—like a lad?" he asked, his concerned gaze lowering to the dark jeans she wore, now splattered with mud. His eyes then swept up to her soaked and dirty T-shirt, lingering on the swell of her breasts. Her face flamed at his appraisal as he continued, "But 'tis quite obvious ye're a lass—and a bonnie one. At least wait till morning tae be on yer way."

Isabelle glowered at him before turning and stalking away. Eventually, she'd hear the sounds of cars or a plane—or *something* that would orient her.

"Where are ye going, lass?" the man demanded, trailing her.

"Away from here," she snapped. "Please stop following me."

To her surprise, he immediately fell back. But she only felt a small semblance of relief as she stumbled forward. The forest only seemed to grow thicker the farther she went. Unease shot through her; she'd not noticed any nearby forests when she'd arrived at Tairseach with Kensa.

And then there was the silence. The eerie silence. There were no distant sounds of cars or planes.

Isabelle stopped, blinking back tears. How could Kensa be so cruel? Isabelle must have passed out and for whatever reason, Kensa dumped her here in the middle of nowhere.

But there was another explanation. Isabelle took a breath, allowing herself to consider the impossible. She'd always told her students when they wrote their creative essays and short stories to always consider the impossible.

She recalled how Kensa had seemed to make the door close on her own, how she seemed to age in real time. She allowed the possibility to sink in, the possibility that Kensa had somehow made her travel back in time, and that large Scot back there had been telling her the truth, and she was indeed in 1390.

She heard a rustling behind her and whirled, screaming when she saw the man standing less than twenty feet behind her.

"I told you not to follow me," she said, placing a hand over her racing heart.

"I never agreed tae that. I just wanted tae make sure ye were safe."

The man's tone was kind, and she softened. She took him in. Even though she'd just met him, there was something trustworthy about the man. Despite the scary sword he carried, she didn't think he meant her any harm.

"I've been camping out here for the night. If ye want tae make camp here as well, I've a cloak for ye tae rest upon. I'll sleep away from ye. Ye'll have nothing tae fear from me," he said gently. "I ken ye want tae leave, but 'tis best not tae travel till first light."

Isabelle swallowed, taking another look around. He was right. She wasn't going anywhere—no matter what year it was—in this darkness.

"Thank you," she murmured.

"I'm called Ciaran," he said. "Ciaran of—" he abruptly stopped himself, and a shadow passed over his face.

"I'm Isabelle," she said, filling the awkward silence.

"Isabelle," he said slowly, and something about the way he said her name made a sharp spike of awareness pierce her. "Allow me tae escort ye back tae my camp."

Isabelle followed him, shaking her head as if to rid herself of the spark of desire she'd felt when he said her name. She'd possibly landed in another time; there was no time to swoon over a mysterious Scot in medieval clothing.

She took several deep breaths to calm herself as they walked. Her brain still protested the notion of having traveled back through time, but there was nothing she could do until she could at least see her surroundings. And then, God willing, she'd find a road—and a way back to Tairseach. Kensa had some answering to do.

They reached a clearing, and Ciaran placed a plaid cloak on the ground by a small fire. He straightened, pointing across the clearing.

"I'll be over there. If ye need food or drink, there's some in that bag over there. If ye want tae get out of yer muddy clothes, I have a fresh tunic in that bag as well. 'Tis long enough that ye can wear it as a gown."

Isabelle nodded her thanks as he made his way across the clearing and out of sight. Once he was gone, she reached into his bag, freezing as she pulled out a tunic. This certainly didn't look like a piece of modern clothing. It looked homemade, but by someone who knew how to stitch well, and made of a comfortable wool fabric.

She shed her dirty clothes and slid on the tunic, settling down onto her makeshift bed. She stared up at the starry night sky, hoping against hope for the sight of a plane or anything that signaled she was still in the twenty-first century. But there were only the multitude of stars and the darkness of the night sky.

There's a reasonable explanation, Isabelle told herself firmly, closing her eyes. *There has to be.*

ISABELLE AWOKE the next morning with a start. She sat up, her body aching from sleeping on the ground. She looked around with a sinking feeling. She'd hoped that it had all been a dream. But she was still in the same clearing, wearing a medieval tunic.

She got to her feet, crossing the clearing to where Ciaran had disappeared to the night before. He could help her get to the nearest road back to Tairseach. But she didn't find him, and for a moment panic filled her as she wondered if he'd left.

She heard splashing in the stream, and her heart soared with relief.

Isabelle followed the sound downstream and froze when she found Ciaran.

Ciaran was cleaning himself off in the stream . . . completely naked. The filth and grime that covered him the night before had hidden a sculpted, muscular body—from a pair of long tapered legs, firm abdominal muscles, broad shoulders, and a rippling back. He was faced away from her, thank God, and didn't seem to notice she was there as he washed himself with his hands.

Isabelle swallowed, wondering how she should make herself known, but she was unable to speak.

Ciaran turned, and the simmering desire that burned within her skyrocketed. The grime and darkness of the night before had concealed not only a stunning body, but a strikingly handsome face. He had a generous mouth, a chiseled jaw dusted with a couple of days' growth of stubble, and an aristocratic nose. He opened his eyes, and Isabelle had to stifle a gasp. His eyes were even more dazzling in daylight—their grays and greens highlighted in the sun. He was by far the most beautiful man she had ever seen.

It was only the look of shock in Ciaran's stunning eyes that brought her back to herself. She turned away from him, swallowing hard.

"I—I'm sorry," she stammered. "I didn't see you when I awoke, so I came to find you."

"'Tis all right, lass," he said, and she could have sworn she heard a trace of amusement in his voice.

A long stretch of silence passed, and she hoped —prayed—that he was getting dressed. Soon, she felt his hand on her shoulder, turning her to face him.

He was even more handsome up close. Those multicolored eyes of his were trained on hers with intense focus. She took a step back, painfully aware of how she must look. Her dark hair was mussed, there were still traces of grime on her skin from the muddy stream, and she must have smelled awful.

"Sorry," she said again, stupidly. She noticed with annoyance that he was only half dressed; he wore a belted plaid kilt, and his glistening muscled abdomen was way too close to her body. She took another step back. "Ah—are you going to put a shirt on?"

He moved past her and shrugged into a tunic he'd strewn over a log. Isabelle expelled a small sigh of relief. At least now she could concentrate.

"Now that it's light," Isabelle said, "can you direct me—or help me find—a road? If I could just—"

"Quiet," Ciaran interrupted, moving to stand in front of her.

Isabelle stilled, startled at his sudden state of alarm.

And then she heard it too. Footsteps approaching them through the trees.

Two men stepped out, their hands on the hilts of their swords, their eyes gleaming with dark intent.

A surge of protectiveness filled Ciaran's chest as the two men approached. By the rough look of them—dirty tunics and torn breeches, bloodshot eyes from the effect of too much drink— he suspected they were bandits. He didn't like the way they were looking at Isabelle, with lasciviousness in their eyes. He moved in front of her to shield her from their gazes.

"If ye leave now, no harm will come tae ye," he said, his hand lowering to the hilt of his sword, relieved that he'd had the sense to place it in its sheath on his belt when he'd dressed.

The men just laughed, taking another menacing step toward them.

"Will ye?" asked the larger of the two, a bearded blond who had the look of a Norseman. "How about we enjoy that lass of yers while ye watch?"

Isabelle let out a terrified whimper behind him,

and rage tore through him. Ciaran took out his sword and charged toward the men with a snarl.

They took out their swords as well, and his weapon clashed with each of theirs. He kicked at the Norseman's knees, sending him sprawling to the ground. He turned his attention to the other man, backing him up to the edge of the clearing as their swords continued to duel. The man let out a ferocious growl and charged toward Ciaran, his sword outstretched, but Ciaran was ready, striking him in the head with the hilt of his sword. The bandit slumped to the ground, still and unconscious.

Ciaran turned to deal with the other bandit, but to his surprise he saw that he lay unconscious at Isabelle's feet. She shakily held the man's sword, her eyes wild with panic.

"He—he came at me," she whispered. "I panicked and grabbed his sword. I just—swung at him."

"Ye did good, lass," he said, giving her an impressed nod. "But we must leave. They'll not stay down long."

She didn't protest, her face still tight with shock as he gathered his things and helped her up onto his horse. After slinging his bag of supplies onto the back of the horse, he climbed on behind her.

Ciaran wrapped his arms around her to get to the reins, a surge of heat coursing through him at the feel of her body against his. He had to force himself to concentrate as he kicked the sides of the horse to gallop out of the clearing. But he remained aware of Isabelle's body against his as they rode out of the forest and onto one of the many green moors that dotted the Highlands.

He veered left when he spotted another patch of forest up ahead, tucked away next to an expanse of rolling hills. From his previous hunting trips, he knew that where there were hills there were caves—perfect hiding spots.

He tugged on the reins, slowing the horse's pace to a trot as they entered the forest. They soon reached a clearing, only steps away from the entrance of a small cave.

Ciaran dismounted, helping Isabelle down before tying the horse to a tree. She remained silent and pale, her arms wrapped around her body. The encounter with the bandits had clearly shaken her.

"Isabelle," he said gently.

She raised her lovely blue eyes to meet his, and he swallowed. He'd been able to tell she was bonnie when he first saw her last night, wet from the stream and illuminated by moonlight, but the darkness had concealed the true strength of her beauty.

Her hair was as dark as a raven's wings, falling in a straight curtain down past her shoulders. Her eyes were the color of the sky at midday, clear and blue. Her features were delicate and feminine—a heart-shaped face, sensual lips, high cheekbones. And beneath the baggy tunic she wore, he could make out the full curve of her breasts, the sensual flare of her hips. Desire shot through his body with the force of an arrow, and he had to take a breath to quell it.

"Ye're safe now, lass," he murmured.

She blinked, seeming to come back to herself at his words.

"Who—who were those men?"

"Bandits," Ciaran said with a sigh. "I've only encountered bandits once before—on a trip south tae Edinburgh. They roam the countryside, stealing from travelers . . . and sometimes worse. 'Tis why I didnae want ye tae wander off on yer own last night."

"It's really the year 1390, isn't it?" she whispered.

He studied her with concern. The lass didn't seem mad, but she spoke her question in earnest.

"Aye," he said.

"Look," she said, taking a shaky step toward him. "I know this is going to sound crazy, but I'm not from this time. That's why I was dressed in those strange clothes. I'm from the twenty-first century—over six hundred years from now. I have no idea how this works—how I got here."

Ciaran stiffened, looking at her with disbelief and suspicion. A sudden dark thought seized him. She'd come out of nowhere—conveniently arriving yards away from his camp. Was she working for his brother? Was she spying on his behalf?

"Are ye working with Tavish?" he demanded. "Did he send ye?"

"I don't know who Tavish is," she snapped. "I'm

telling you the truth. I'm not from this time and I need to get back. Do—do you know where Tairseach is? Is it nearby?"

"I've never heard of the place," Ciaran said, his eyes still narrowed with suspicion.

But . . . her fear and frustration seemed genuine. And Tavish had always dismissed lasses and their intelligence. He would never allow a lass to spy for him.

But while he could believe she wasn't working for Tavish, he certainly didn't believe her wild story.

"Please," Isabelle whispered, desperation filling her eyes. "You don't have to believe me, and I don't blame you for that. But can you at least help me get back to Tairseach? Or—or point me in the right direction?"

He sighed. Even though she was telling him a false tale, his honor wouldn't allow him to let her travel on her own.

"I'm camping here for the night tae make certain those bandits doonae pick up our trail and follow. Then I plan tae go tae the manor of a friend. He may ken of this village ye speak of and can have someone escort ye there."

Isabelle closed her eyes, her shoulders sinking with relief. He surveyed her tense expression, wondering what the lass was truly hiding.

It doesnae matter. He had no time to get involved in her plight, whatever it was. He needed to get to Gabhran's manor and make a plan to clear his name and return home. Gabhran would send this strange lass on her way.

"I'll set up an area in that cave for ye tae sleep," he said. "'Tis not ideal, but 'tis for the best. And the only rations I have for the rest of the day are bread and ale."

"It's fine," she said, smiling. She reached out to touch his arm, and heat careened through him at her touch. "Thank you, Ciaran."

He gave her a quick nod, stepping out of her grasp. A flash of hurt crossed her face at his evasion, one she quickly masked.

"So . . .where are you from?" she asked. "Is your home nearby?"

He stiffened. He was afraid she'd ask probing questions; he had no intention of telling her he was an outlaw. Especially given her own false story.

"I'm just traveling in this area," he said shortly.

He turned to leave before she could ask any more questions, heading into the cave.

The cave was larger than it looked from the outside; there was more than enough room for the both of them. He gathered some fallen branches and sticks by the entrance, carrying them inside.

"Is there anything I can do to help?" Isabelle asked.

"I can handle it, lass," he said, focused on stacking wood for the fire.

"May—may I ask you something?" she hedged, after a brief silence. "Have you heard of a Fiona, by any chance? Fiona Stewart?"

"There are many Fionas in the Highlands," he said, looking up at her with a puzzled frown. "I ken two Fionas—one a wee lass in her ninth year, the other an elderly cook."

Disappointment flashed across her face.

"Who is she?" he asked.

"My closest friend. She's like a sister," she said, her voice wavering. "It's why I may have been sent here—to this time."

Ciaran's mouth tightened, but he said nothing. The lass was determined to stick to her tale. He quickly got the fire started and stood.

"I'll be in the clearing gathering more firewood," he said, not looking at her as he stepped out of the cave.

As he worked, gathering any stray sticks he could find, a memory struck him. The last time he'd built a fire was during a hunting trip with Eoin a few months ago. They'd gone on a hunt in the forests that surrounded Aitharne Castle and had made camp there for the day. The stressors of his duties as laird had taken their toll on Ciaran, and Eoin insisted he needed a break. They'd invited Tavish to come along, but he'd declined.

"I doonae ken why he dislikes me so," Ciaran had said, with a heavy sigh.

"He's always kept tae himself. He doesnae like anyone," Eoin had returned, with a dismissive wave of his hand.

Ciaran had fallen silent. Eoin was right, Tavish had always kept to himself and didn't seem to have close ties to anyone—including his brothers. But Tavish had seemed more remote and isolated than usual, not even coming to suppers in the great hall, taking his meals alone in his chamber.

Just weeks later, Eoin would be dead by Tavish's hand.

Ciaran paused from his task, closing his eyes as a wave of anger and grief roiled through him.

"I'll avenge ye, Eoin," he whispered into the silence.

A twig snapped behind him and he whirled, his hand lowering to the hilt of his sword. But it was Isabelle who stood there, hands up, giving him an apologetic look.

"I'm sorry. I didn't mean to startle you."

He turned, resuming his task, hating that she'd caught him in a state of vulnerability. Had she heard what he said?

"I just wanted to tell you—the fire in the cave is already dying."

When he returned to the cave to tend to it, Isabelle knelt down by his side.

"Let me help," she said. Her proximity was unnerving; he could see the curve of her breasts beneath her tunic. "I insist. I hate being useless."

He grudgingly showed her how to use a fire steel to restart the fire, and he had her use torn fabric from his bag as kindling to ignite the flames.

As the fire roared to life, he glanced up, admiring the curve of her long neck and the bright blue of her eyes, illuminated by the flames. For just a moment, he forgot about his ever-present grief and guilt, as something he'd not experienced in a long while coursed through him.

Desire. In his mind's eye, he saw himself tasting the tender flesh of Isabelle's lips, pressing her body to his as he explored her mouth.

Isabelle stilled as her blue eyes met his, as if aware of his lustful thoughts. He could have sworn he saw her eyes darken with the same molten desire that filled his body.

But he forced his gaze away from hers, getting to his feet.

"I'll be out gathering more wood," he said gruffly, turning to leave, though his desire still burned as fierce as the fire that now raged inside the cave.

Ciaran remained silent for the rest of the day, only giving her one-word replies whenever she asked him a question. Isabelle wondered if she'd imagined that brief, heated moment when his eyes had lingered on her lips, and she'd thought he might kiss her.

She'd wanted him to. Badly. She was ashamed of herself for this; she shouldn't be at all focused on her attraction to the strikingly handsome Scot.

Isabelle took a bite out of the bread that would serve as her supper, looking around at the dark cave. Evening had fallen, and she was alone in the cave, Ciaran was right outside. He'd told her he wanted to keep watch in case any more bandits stumbled upon their camp, but she doubted this was the case. She suspected he was avoiding her.

A stab of hurt pricked her at the thought, but she ignored it, turning her thoughts to Kensa. Kensa was responsible for her coming to this time, though she wasn't sure how. At first, she'd thought she should just get back to Tairseach and figure out how to get back from there.

But then she'd thought of Fiona. Kensa had said Fiona didn't belong in the present—and neither did she. Isabelle could only deduce that Kensa had done the same thing to Fiona that she'd done to Isabelle—and sent her back to the past.

She recalled the letter that Fiona had sent her, scrawled out on parchment that could have definitely come from this time. If Fiona was in 1390, Isabelle was determined to find her. It had already proven to be a dangerous time for a woman here— what would Isabelle have done had those bandits come upon her alone? If Fiona was here, God only knew what had happened to her. If Isabelle could find her, she could get them both back to the present. Somehow.

She glanced back at Ciaran, who sat by the entrance to the cave, his back to her as he drank his ale and nibbled on his bread in silence. Perhaps this friend he was taking her to would know something. Even if there were many Fionas in Scotland, wouldn't her Fiona, a woman with a modern American accent, stand out?

As if sensing her gaze, Ciaran turned around to face her, training those stunning hazel eyes on her. Embarrassed, Isabelle averted her gaze, but Ciaran stood and entered the cave, taking a seat opposite her.

"I want tae apologize, lass," he said. "I feel I've

been tae harsh tae ye. Things havenae been easy for me as of late. I may not believe yer story, but I hope my friend can have ye escorted safely tae Tairseach."

He smiled, and heat spiraled through her. She lowered her gaze, deciding not to mention that she intended to stay here to find Fiona—though she had no idea how.

"Thank you," she said instead.

"Ye can sleep in here for the night," he said, clambering to his feet. "I'm going tae sleep out by the entrance tae make certain no one rides by."

"Won't it be better if you stay out of sight?" Isabelle asked with a concerned frown. "If those bandits find us—"

"I'm a light sleeper, lass," he said. "I'd wake before they could even strike."

He left her alone, and Isabelle tried to make herself comfy on the makeshift bed of Ciaran's cloak, her thoughts straying back to Fiona. How would she find her in the proverbial haystack of the medieval Scottish Highlands? And how could she even be certain Fiona was even in this time?

When Isabelle finally drifted off to sleep, it was with these unanswered questions circling throughout her mind.

ISABELLE AWOKE in the middle of the night to the sound of moans and whimpers. She sat up, alarmed, until she realized they were coming from the cave entrance. Ciaran.

She sat up and hurried toward the entrance. Ciaran lay on his side, his large body shaking as he let out pained moans.

"Please—" Ciaran whimpered. "Eoin—"

Her heart clenched in sympathy. Isabelle knelt down, reaching out to gently shake his shoulder.

Ciaran awoke instantly, sitting up, his hazel eyes wild as he looked around, before his gaze settled on her.

"You were having a nightmare," she said.

Ciaran closed his eyes, pressing his hands to his temples.

"I—I'm sorry I woke ye, lass," he muttered.

"It's all right," Isabelle said. She bit her lip, studying him. "I know we just met . . . but I'm a good listener. Who's Eoin?"

He flinched, averting his gaze.

"I doonae want tae plague ye with my problems, lass."

"Well, at least come back inside," she said, standing and extending her hand. The night air was chilly and pricked at her skin. "It's much warmer."

He looked like he would protest, but after a moment he took her hand and stood.

Isabelle wasn't prepared for the surge of fire that filled her at his touch, and she removed her hand from his as he followed her back into the recesses of the cave.

"Eoin was my brother."

Isabelle turned to face him, startled. He stood by the fire, gazing down at the flames.

"He died," he continued, his voice wavering. "It—was my fault."

"How was it your fault?" Isabelle asked, empathy filling her at the guilt and heartbreak on Ciaran's face.

"He was murdered," Ciaran whispered. "I should have protected him."

"No. The person who killed your brother is the one responsible—and only him. Grief is enough to deal with. There's no need to add guilt to the burden."

Ciaran gave her a sad smile, lifting his eyes from the fire to meet hers.

"If only it were that simple, lass. Tae let go of the guilt. I fear I cannae."

"You can try," she said. "I—I feel guilt over someone I've lost as well," she continued, thinking of Fiona. "But I'm making myself take action and move forward. It's the only way—the best way—to let the guilt go."

Ciaran studied her, and awareness and desire sparked beneath her skin as the silence stretched between them. He looked angelically beautiful in the light of the fire, his chiseled features and hazel eyes even more pronounced. His gaze lowered to her lips, and Isabelle's mouth went dry.

There was no mistaking the raw flare of desire in his eyes as he stepped closer to her, so they were only inches apart. Something different infused the silence now . . . temptation and need. Lust.

Ciaran reached out to touch the side of her face, and the sparks of desire turned into a fiery wave that seized her. He leaned down, pressing his lips to hers, pulling her body flush against his.

His tongue explored her mouth, and Isabelle let out a moan as his hand lowered to her nape, holding her close to him. He tasted of the bitter ale he'd just consumed, but to Isabelle it might as well have been a sweet nectar. She could feel every inch of him pressed close to her—the broad expanse of his muscular torso, and the growing evidence of his arousal.

But all too quickly it was over. Ciaran released her with abrupt swiftness, stepping back.

"I—I shouldnae have done that," he muttered, turning away from her. "I'm sorry, lass."

And before she could protest, still breathless from his kiss, he was gone.

CHAPTER 8

"We'll need tae be on our way," Ciaran said, not looking at Isabelle as he addressed her. "And ye'll need tae come up with another story besides being from six centuries ahead. My friends are kind, but ye'll only make them suspicious with a tale like that."

It was early the next morning, just after first light, and he'd entered the cave to speak to Isabelle. He'd barely been able to sleep after kissing her, the memory of her warm curves pressed against his body, and her soft lips opening to his, haunting his mind.

But guilt filled him over his lustful thoughts. He had no right to desire, to pleasure, while his innocent brother rotted in the ground and his murderer roamed free.

The thought hardened his resolve, and he finally looked at Isabelle. She looked even lovelier than she had the night before in the soft firelight of the cave; the loose tunic she wore had slipped, revealing the seductive curve of her shoulders. *Damn me,* he thought with frustration. *The lass gets bonnier by the day.*

"Fine. Even though I am telling the truth," Isabelle said with a stubborn jut of her lovely chin. "I'll just say that I was traveling through the Highlands and then set upon by bandits. You rescued me. That part is true."

"Good," he said, though he gritted his teeth at her stubborn insistence of her false tale. "I'm certain Gabhran will be happy tae help ye arrange transport tae this village ye speak of."

"Your friends—are they familiar with surrounding villages? Do they know other clans?" Isabelle asked suddenly. At his questioning look, she continued, "I'm hoping that they've maybe heard word of my friend Fiona."

"Aye. But doonae wear much on their kindness," Ciaran cautioned, giving her a wary look. "'Tis enough that I'm showing my face on their property."

"Why?" Isabelle asked with a puzzled frown. "I thought you were their friend."

Ciaran stilled; he'd said too much. She didn't know he was an outlaw, a former laird and chieftain accused of murdering his brother. A sudden tightness gripped his chest. How would she look at him if she knew? Would she be disgusted by the knowledge that she'd allowed an outlaw to kiss her?

"I just doonae wish tae hinder them. I'm

arriving unannounced," he said shortly. "We need tae leave," he added, before she could question him further.

To his relief she didn't press him, and moments later they were riding out of the forest and back toward the countryside. As they rode, he had to force himself to concentrate on the landscape ahead, to distract himself from the feel of her body against his and her natural sweet scent that filled his nostrils. She was too much of a temptation; once she was on her way, he'd have his bearings again.

Gabhran's manor was located in the western Highlands, and they rode for some time to get there. Whenever he spotted a lone horse or carriage on a distant road, he slowed down the pace of his horse to avoid any interception. He could tell that this drew Isabelle's curiosity every time he did this, as she cast curious glances over her shoulder at him.

"I'm not certain if they're bandits," he said by explanation, after the third time he'd slowed down the pace of his horse. She gave him a nod, but by the lingering look she gave him, he knew she remained suspicious.

Frustration coursed through him; he hated having to live like this. He'd only known life as a respectable man, as a well-liked laird and chief of his clan. But until he cleared his name, this was how his life would have to be.

It was midday when they reached Gabhran's lands; his stone manor loomed in the distance like a comforting beacon, and Ciaran's tension ebbed away. But his calm was short-lived; his brother knew Gabhran was a close and loyal friend to Ciaran. How did he know his brother hadn't already sent men here?

He surveyed the grounds around the manor, looking for any hint of Tavish or his men as they approached the courtyard. But no one looked menacing or suspicious; the few servants who milled about the grounds only cast him and Isabelle looks of mild curiosity.

It was Gabhran himself who emerged from the front doors of the manor, and relief filled him at the sight of Gabhran's full and stout frame, his auburn hair, his kind brown eyes. His wife Donella trailed out after Gabhran, and she gave Ciaran a wide smile.

But their looks of welcoming faltered when their gazes strayed to Isabelle. Ciaran turned to face her, a look of warning in his eyes. She was not to tell her friends her strange tale. Seeming to understand his meaning, she jerked her head in a nod.

As he dismounted, helping Isabelle down, Gabhran approached.

"Ciaran. This is a surprise. What brings ye here?"

"There's much I need tae tell ye," Ciaran said, lowering his voice. Gabhran frowned with concern, as Ciaran continued, "Let us talk inside."

~

"Christ," Gabhran whispered, taking a large swig of ale, handing a second cup to Ciaran, which he took with gratitude.

They were in his study, Isabelle having gone with Donella to wash up and change into more appropriate clothing. Ciaran had told him everything that happened from the time of his arrest until now.

"The bastard," Gabhran continued, shaking his head. "I always knew there was something dark about yer brother, but I never thought . . ."

Relief swept over Ciaran; he'd feared Gabhran may have thought he was guilty. Gabhran seemed to read his thoughts, giving him a dark scowl.

"If ye think for a moment I thought ye capable of murdering yer own flesh and blood, I'll take a swing at ye," Gabhran growled. "Ye've not a murderous bone in yer body, and the nobles in yer clan are fools for nae seeing what yer brother is doing."

"He has witnesses," Ciaran muttered. "Witnesses I've no doubt he bribed."

Gabhran swore a violent curse, slamming his ale down onto the table.

"What can I do tae help?"

"First, I'll have ye ken—I'm not staying here. 'Tis only a matter of time before my brother sends his men here, and I'll not make ye and yer family a target."

"I'm not afeared of yer brother; he's always been afeared of me," Gabhran returned. "Ye're staying here until we clear yer name and return ye tae yer castle."

"Gabhran—"

"Yer staying here or I'll report ye tae yer brother myself," Gabhran said firmly, and Ciaran couldn't help but smile. He was just as stubborn—and loyal—as Lachaid.

"Aye," Ciaran said. "But if I get any hint that my presence has put ye in danger . . ."

"Do ye have a plan?" Gabhran asked, waving off his words.

"I need allies. Spies tae go back tae the castle and get evidence of my brother's treachery. And I need his witnesses to recant their false testimonies."

As he spoke the words aloud, Ciaran realized how difficult this would be, and a sudden uncertainty pierced him.

"But Tavish will be closely watching anyone loyal tae me," Ciaran continued with frustration, raking his hand through his hair.

"That's why ye have me. I'm out of yer brother's reach. I'm loyal tae ye, and my men are loyal tae ye. They'll help," Gabhran said. "I'll call a meeting with the ones I trust the most."

A rush of gratitude filled Ciaran, and he gave his friend a nod of thanks. Like Lachaid, he'd known Gabhran since he was a bairn. He and Lachaid were the only two who'd shown him true friendship or kindness since Tavish had him thrown in the dungeons of his own castle.

"Now," Gabhran said, his eyes twinkling with

mischief. "Are ye going tae tell me about the lass ye came here with? Is she a Sassenach? Never heard one who speaks the way she does."

"Aye," Ciaran said. He had his suspicions about Isabelle's strange accent as well. He recalled her insistent words back in the forest. *I'm not from this time.* But he pushed away the thought.

"She was traveling through these parts tae visit family and was separated from her escort. Bandits set upon her, I helped her get away from them."

He hoped Gabhran wouldn't ask more questions about her, but he continued to study Ciaran, cocking his head to the side.

"She's quite a bonnie lass," he said with a sly look.

"I did what any honorable man would do. I helped her," Ciaran said shortly. *And tasted her.* The memory of Isabelle's soft moan as he kissed her filled his mind, and he looked away from Gabhran's discerning gaze. "I mentioned tae ye earlier that she'll need transport. She wants tae go tae a village by the name of Tairseach. Have ye heard of it?"

Gabhran stilled at the mention of Tairseach, the playful look in his eyes vanishing.

"Tairseach?" he echoed.

"Aye," Ciaran said, studying him closely. "What is it, Gabhran? Have ye heard of it?"

"'Tis just an abandoned village from what I've heard," Gabhran said. "I doonae ken why she'd want tae go there."

Ciaran eyed him. Gabhran was hiding something. And if Tairseach was an abandoned village, why would Isabelle want to go there? But he shook his head; it was none of his concern.

"I doonae ken. But I told the lass ye may be able tae help. Can ye arrange transport?"

"I can have a trusted rider escort her north," Gabhran said. After a pause, his face lit up with a mischievous grin. "Why are ye so eager tae rid yerself of the bonnie lass?"

"I've enough tae handle without a wayward lass on my hands," Ciaran said, ignoring the odd sense of loss that filled him at the thought of Isabelle's departure. "Now tell me more about these men of yers who'll help me clear my name."

CHAPTER 9

"Where did ye get such odd clothes?" Donella breathed.

Isabelle stood in the center of a large guest chamber, her arms wrapped self-consciously around herself. Donella, a pretty brunette with warm brown eyes, stood opposite her, supervising a chambermaid who helped Isabelle get changed.

Isabelle already had to insist she could wash herself, but Donella practically ordered her to stand still and allow the chambermaid to dress her. The women of this time weren't as shy about nudity as Isabelle had thought; neither of the women seemed to care that Isabelle stood in nothing but her bra and underwear.

Now, both Donella and the maid studied her lacy bra and underwear as if they were something out of a horror movie. If she weren't so freaked out by the situation she was in, it would be amusing. Isabelle was tempted to tell Donella she'd bought them at a Victoria's Secret store in Chicago, but resisted the urge.

After Donella had looked at her strangely given her accent, she'd told Donella the story she'd rehearsed with Ciaran, that she was a wayward traveler from England set upon by bandits. What was one more lie?

"I made these myself," she said. "I find them comfortable."

"Aye?" Donella asked, eyeing Isabelle's bra. "I mean no offense, but this looks like something a whore would wear." She gestured to the maid, who approached her with a lightweight underdress.

"No offense taken," Isabelle said with a polite smile. "It's why I wear it beneath my clothes."

She stepped out of her bra and underwear and slipped into the underdress, assisted by the maid.

"Such lovely skin," Donella marveled, and relief filled Isabelle. She'd feared Donella would ask her for details on how to stitch a bra and underwear. "Most lasses around our age have marks from plague or other sickness, even the nobles. Do ye never get sick, lass?"

Isabelle bit her lip as the maid helped her into a white tunic, and then into a light blue gown. She was in a time before advanced medicine and vaccinations. It was easy to forget things like this about the past. She was no historian, but she could hasten a guess that many people who survived into adulthood would have some visible bout with illness.

"I've been blessed with good health," Isabelle said hastily.

"Ye certainly have," Donella said. She took in Isabelle's clothing, giving her a nod of approval and dismissing the maid with a wave of her hand. "There. Now ye look respectable. Have a look at yerself."

Donella gestured to a mirror in the far corner of the chamber, and Isabelle went to it, taking in her reflection. The medieval gown, with its long sleeves, delicately cut bodice and comfortable wool fabric suited her. If it weren't for her hair, still damp from the washing she'd given it, which she now wore loose about her shoulders, she would look exactly like a fourteenth-century noble woman.

Oh my God, Isabelle thought, her heart hammering wildly against her rib cage. *I truly am in the past.*

"Thank you," Isabelle said finally. "For the clothes. They're lovely."

"'Tis not a bother," Donella said. "This will be yer chamber while ye're here. Ciaran mentioned that ye'll need transport?"

Isabelle hesitated. How could she casually mention that she wanted to stay to look for Fiona?

"If—if you don't mind, I'd like to stay for a bit. Or—at least as long as Ciaran is here," she hedged, not knowing how Ciaran would react to this bit of news.

To her surprise, Donella didn't look put out by

her words. Instead, a look of delight spread across her face.

"I'd always hoped Ciaran would find a lass that made him happy. I wondered about the two of ye, given the way he was looking at ye when ye arrived, but now I am—"

"Oh—no," Isabelle interjected, flushing. "It's not like that. He just rescued me, that's all. The truth is . . . I'm looking for someone. That's why I came here. From—from England," she babbled.

"Ah," Donella said, the disappointment in her eyes plain. "Who are ye looking for?"

"My sister," Isabelle lied. She hoped a missing sister would foster more sympathy than a missing friend. "Her name is Fiona. Fiona Stewart."

"What clan?" Donella asked. "Is she a noble? A peasant woman?"

Frustration filled Isabelle's gut. There was no middle class in this time; you were either a peasant or wealthy. And Isabelle had no idea what Fiona was up to in this time. *If she's even in this time*, she reminded herself.

"I'm not sure," Isabelle said. "We've lost touch."

"I'm sorry tae hear. There are many lasses in the Highlands by the name of Fiona—noble and peasant alike. I'm not certain me and my husband can help ye find her."

Isabelle's heart sank. She knew this would likely be the case, but that didn't stop her disappointment.

How was she supposed to even begin searching for Fiona? Perhaps it was a lost cause after all.

"But if ye tell me what she looks like, I can have a messenger ride tae the nearby villages and ask around," Donella said, studying Isabelle's pained face with sympathy.

"Thank you," Isabelle said with a sliver of hope. It was still a needle in a haystack approach, but it was a start.

"Mama!"

Isabelle turned as a little girl, a miniature version of Donella, flew into the room. Donella's expression filled with love and she knelt down to embrace her.

"This is my wee bairn, Annis," Donella said, beaming.

"Nice to meet you, Annis," Isabelle said, smiling at the adorable girl, who gave her a shy smile.

"I'm going tae take this wee one back tae her chamber. I'll see ye later for supper," Donella said, taking Annis's hand and leaving the room.

Once she was alone, Isabelle moved to the window, looking out over the vast moors that stretched beyond the manor. For the first time since she'd arrived here, a sense of awe settled over her.

She was in the year 1390. It was still almost a century until Columbus's discovery of the Americas. As a lover of classic literature, she marveled over the fact that William Shakespeare's birth was still two centuries ahead. Geoffrey Chaucer was still alive in this time. Other events she'd learned about in history class—the Tudors, the French Revolution, the American Civil War—all had yet to come.

Was Fiona indeed in this time as well? If so, what was she doing? And most importantly—was she safe?

"Isabelle."

The rumble of Ciaran's voice pulled Isabelle from her thoughts, and she turned.

Ciaran stood in the doorway; her breath hitched in her throat at the sight of him. He was also cleaned up, looking breathtakingly handsome in a fresh white tunic and dark green plaid kilt. He entered the chamber, and heat rushed through her as his hazel eyes swept over her from head to toe. She realized this was the first time he'd seen her in era-appropriate clothing.

"Ye look bonnie in a lady's clothes," he murmured.

"Thank you," Isabelle said, flushing at his appraisal.

"Donella just told me ye want tae stay as long as I'm here? Tae find yer friend?"

"I didn't mean to involve you," Isabelle said quickly. "Your friends seem very kind, but I don't think they'd be willing to host a stranger on their own. And I told her Fiona's my sister," she added with a guilty flush. "It just seemed more likely they'd help if she was my sister—and if I was with you. I'll stay out of your way, I promise. I just want to find Fiona."

Isabelle held her breath as she waited for his response, fearful that he would refuse.

"'Tis fine," he said, after a brief pause, and her shoulders sank with relief. "But I should remind ye—I'm hoping tae not be here for long."

Isabelle studied him, wondering why Ciaran was so wary about staying here for long. She suspected he was hiding something from her; she still didn't know what he was doing in the forest when she first stumbled upon him. She hadn't bought his vague "traveling" story. For some reason, his dishonesty hurt. She'd been nothing but honest with him; even if he didn't believe her story.

"'Tis quite the view," he murmured, his words again pulling her from the maelstrom of her thoughts. He was staring past her out the window, and she turned to follow his gaze. "When I was a wee lad, I'd look out the window and see the moors stretching into the horizon. I imagined mounting a horse and seeing if I could ride till I reached where the cliffs met the sea. The lands seemed so grand when I was a bairn."

Isabelle smiled, taken by the boyish wonder in his eyes.

"They are grand," she agreed.

"Isabelle," he said, after a brief pause. "I wanted tae apologize again, for kissing ye last night. I shouldnae have—"

"It's fine," she interrupted, another stab of hurt piercing her. Why did he feel the need to apologize for the best kiss she'd ever had? "There's no need to apologize. Really."

Ciaran hesitated, his eyes probing hers, and Isabelle had to look away. She was suddenly hyper-aware that they were alone in a bed chamber. A brief, scandalous image of Ciaran carrying her to the large bed in the center of the room, tearing off her clothes and kissing every part of her body filled her mind, and her heartbeat picked up its pace.

When she met Ciaran's eyes again, they had darkened, and she wondered—hoped—that despite his apology, he would kiss her again. But instead, he took a step back from her.

"I'll see ye for supper," he said, turning to leave the room.

Isabelle watched him go, the hurt that pierced her earlier flaring into an ache. Why did Ciaran's distance bother her so much? She was here for one reason and one reason only; to find Fiona. She'd just have to focus on keeping the distractingly handsome man out of her thoughts.

CHAPTER 10

"I've kent Ciaran since he was just a lad," Gabhran said. "Got him out of many a scrape."

Isabelle sat with Ciaran, Gabhran, and Donella in a large ornate dining room over a supper of roasted pork, vegetables, and ale.

Isabelle didn't realize how hungry she was until she'd started eating. While the bread she'd eaten with Ciaran in the wilderness had been somewhat filling, it certainly hadn't been tasty, and Isabelle now savored every bite of her meal.

She set down her spoon, turning to look at Ciaran with a smile. An adorable flush had spread across his cheeks at Gabhran's words.

"And I got ye out of many a scrape as well," Ciaran said, taking a swig of his ale. "Donella would've never accepted yer proposal if it wasnae for me."

"'Tis true," Donella said, laughing. "I'd have

never taken such a louse as husband without Ciaran's kind words."

"Ah, ye betray me, wife," Gabhran said, looking at Donella with such love that Isabelle felt a rush of envy. She'd assumed that most if not all marriages in this time were arrangements for reasons of property or politics, but in the brief time she'd been around Gabhran and Donella, she could see how much they genuinely loved each other.

Isabelle's own love life was nonexistent. She'd envied her brother Scott's happy marriage to his wife, Jane. They'd been together for as long as Isabelle could remember, and she could see how happy Jane made him. Isabelle's longest relationship had lasted for a year to a fellow teacher; she'd been the one to end it. There had been nothing wrong with Greg—she'd just found their relationship excruciatingly boring. All the brief relationships she'd had since then had simply come and gone, and Isabelle assumed that whomever she ended up settling down with—if she ended up settling down at all—would be a man she was good friends with, and with whom she shared a mild attraction. After all, Scott had once told her that friendships were the basis of every good long-term marriage.

"But don't you feel a spark for Jane?" Isabelle had asked Scott.

"Every day," he'd replied with a smile. "There's a quote out there that says love is friendship set on fire. I like to think desire is included in that as well."

Fire. Her eyes strayed to Ciaran as she thought of their explosive kiss in the cave, of the heat that seared her skin at his mere touch. Ciaran met her gaze, something unreadable lurking in the hazel depths of his eyes.

"How did you and Ciaran meet?" Isabelle asked Gabhran, tearing her eyes away from Ciaran's and taking a sip of her ale.

"Our fathers were allies in times of conflict—as well as our clans. At first I didnae like Ciaran. He was single-minded, only focused on the fact that he was the *tainistear*; heir to the chieftain."

"Ye wasnae so pleasant yerself," Ciaran returned. His tone was light and teasing, but his expression had tightened.

"I did like yer brother Eoin as soon as I met him," Gabhran said, his eyes thoughtful. "Kind lad. But Tavish—"

"Doonae say his name," Ciaran spat, gripping the edge of the table so tightly his knuckles turned white. "After what he's done, I never want his name uttered around me again."

Ciaran's words shattered the light mood. Isabelle stilled, taking in Ciaran's fierce expression with surprise.

"Ye're right," Gabhran said, holding his hands up in a gesture of contrition. "After what the bastard did tae ye—murdering yer brother and setting ye up for it—"

"That's enough," Ciaran growled. He shot to his

feet and stalked from the room, leaving a strained silence in his wake.

Gabhran and Donella exchanged a worried look. Isabelle stared at Ciaran's empty chair, frozen. So that's what Ciaran was hiding. He was an outlaw, and the brother he grieved, whom he called out for in his nightmares—had been murdered. By his own flesh and blood.

Isabelle's heart clenched with both horror and sympathy. She'd only known Ciaran briefly, but the man exuded nothing but kindness and honor. There wasn't a doubt in her mind that he was innocent.

Isabelle got to her feet to go after him.

"Lass, perhaps 'tis best tae let him go," Gabhran said gently.

But Isabelle didn't heed his words. She left the dining room, spotting Ciaran striding down the long hallway, but she trailed him from a distance as he made his way out the back doors of the manor.

Isabelle followed him outside, finding him standing before the rear gardens, gazing out at the darkening countryside. He didn't turn around when she stepped outside, but he seemed to sense her presence.

"Go back inside, Isabelle," he muttered.

"No," Isabelle said. She stepped forward until she stood next to him, studying his handsome profile in the darkness.

"You didn't have to hide that from me. I may

not have known you for long, but I can tell you're not a murderer."

"And why is that?" Ciaran asked, turning to look down at her, his eyes narrowed. He advanced, his eyes darkening, and she instinctively took a step back. "How do ye ken I'm not responsible for my brother's death?"

"Because you loved him. I can tell by the way you spoke of him. How you cried out for him in your nightmare," she said, unfazed by his harsh words. "That wasn't a murderer's guilt—it was grief. I have a brother too. He's my only living family. I'd be devastated if I lost him. I can only imagine what you're going through."

The darkness in Ciaran's eyes vanished, replaced by a look of raw vulnerability.

"Well, now ye ken," he said, looking away from her. "I'm an outlaw. My brother has men looking for me. 'Tis best if ye go yer own way, lass, and keep yer distance from me. I'm a wanted man."

"A wanted man who saved my life," Isabelle returned. "A wanted man who protected me when he didn't have to."

Ciaran hesitated, giving her a smile that was both rueful—and wolfish.

"My intentions werenae altogether honorable, lass," he said, his voice dropping to a whisper. "Even in those strange and dirty clothes, ye were the bonniest lass I'd ever laid eyes upon."

Isabelle's face flamed as his gaze probed hers.

He reached out to touch the side of her face, and desire coiled through her at his touch.

"For a moment—just a moment—all my sorrows went away at the sight of ye," he continued, his voice husky. "All I can think of is how much I want another taste of ye."

Isabelle's heart pounded with such ferocity that she could hear it thundering in her ears. Ciaran tilted her face up to his, and she was unable to breathe as he leaned down to seize her lips in a kiss.

The fiery heat of desire filled Ciaran's body as he held Isabelle close, probing her mouth with his. She tasted just as sweet as he remembered from their kiss in the cave, and he couldn't stop the pleasured growl that emitted from his lips at the taste of her.

He released her only when they were breathless, and tilted her head back to nip at the base of her throat. Her skin was even softer there, her natural honeyed scent more potent.

"Ciaran . . ." Isabelle expelled his name with a sigh. The sound of his name on her lips made him harden against his kilt, and he seized her lips once more. This time Isabelle reached up to wind her hands through his hair, pressing his body firmly against her own.

The world around him faded away as he explored Isabelle's mouth. Her hardened nipples grazed his tunic, and he ached to lower her bodice and suckle them into his mouth. He groaned into her mouth at the thought, wanting the barrier of their clothing to fade away, to feel the softness of her bare skin against his, to kiss the plane of her abdomen until he reached the juncture in between her thighs, where he would take his time delving into her sweetness.

His cock strained against his kilt at the images roiling through his mind. He released her mouth, burying his face into the silken softness of her hair. Never had he ached for a lass as he ached for Isabelle; it took every bit of his control to not make love to her right there in the garden.

Ciaran forced himself to step back from her, averting his gaze from the picture of loveliness she made—her lips plump from his kisses, her blue eyes infused with desire. He took her hand, and even that simple act filled him with yet another surge of need.

He led her back inside the manor, stroking the inside of her wrist with his thumb as they walked, her pulse leaping and fluttering beneath his touch. When they reached her chamber door, he lifted her hand and pressed it to his lips.

"Good night, bonnie Isabelle," he murmured.

She met his eyes, and he could see her disappointment which she unsuccessfully tried to hide with a polite smile.

"Good night."

Isabelle stepped into her chamber, shutting the door behind her. Ciaran closed his eyes. Despite his desire for her, he wouldn't ensnare her with an outlaw. She was an innocent lass, here in Scotland to find her friend—which he believed, even if he didn't believe her fanciful story about coming from the future.

He turned and made himself walk away from her chamber before his cock made a different decision for him.

Images of Isabelle dominated his dreams that night. Her dark hair glistening in the moonlight of the garden, her soft lips against his, her generous curves pressed close to his body.

But when those pleasurable images faded, darker ones replaced them, images that had haunted him since Eoin's death. He saw Eoin's still lifeless body, his eyes wide and unseeing, and Ciaran awoke with a strangled gasp.

He looked around, his breath ragged. It was just past first light; early morning sunlight illuminated the chamber. Ciaran leaned back against his pillows, guilt skittering through him. He shouldn't be dreaming of Isabelle, not when he should only be thinking of Eoin and avenging his murder.

He avoided Isabelle's gaze at the morning meal, though he allowed himself a quick glance; not looking at her was like trying to avoid the sun's rays on a midsummer's day. Her eyes met his across the long table, and a tumult of longing and desire coursed through him. He had to force himself to look away.

If Gabhran and Donella noticed anything

strange about his and Isabelle's behavior, they said nothing, keeping the conversation light, but Gabhran slid perceptive looks between the two of them.

He and Gabhran excused themselves after the meal, and he felt Isabelle's gaze on his retreating back.

Once they were alone in Gabhran's study, Ciaran closed the door behind them.

"I want tae apologize," he said gruffly. "For last night. I didnae mean tae lose my temper. I didnae want Isabelle tae ken I'm an outlaw."

"Ye care for the lass," Gabhran said. It was an observation, not a question.

Ciaran hesitated. He thought of the feel of Isabelle in his arms last night, and in the cave. He desired her in a way he'd never desired anyone, but he told himself he didn't know Isabelle well enough for his feelings to run deeper.

"She's a bonnie lass," Ciaran replied, averting his gaze from Gabhran's perceptive one.

"Last night after supper I went to find ye," Gabhran said, not swayed by Ciaran's evasiveness. "I saw ye two in the garden."

Ciaran stilled. From the mischievous glint in Gabhran's eyes, he must have seen him kissing Isabelle.

"It was not a surprise," Gabhran continued, smiling. "I see the way she looks at ye. And ye at her."

"I desire Isabelle, aye. But nothing further will

happen between us," Ciaran said firmly, though he was just trying to convince himself. "She'll be on her way tae Tairseach after yer messenger completes his search for Fiona."

Gabhran's expression tightened when he mentioned Tairseach, and Ciaran froze. He studied his friend.

"Gabhran," he said. "What is it ye ken about Tairseach?"

"Do ye remember my Aunt Ilka?" Gabhran asked, after a brief moment of hesitation.

"Aye," Ciaran said, his lips twitching in amusement. Ilka had been an odd woman, mumbling to herself at all times and insisting that he and Gabhran sit on her lap so she could sing to them. He, Gabhran, and other bairns had gone out of their way to avoid her.

"Well, she would go on about Tairseach anytime me and my family went tae visit her. She would insist that people appeared and disappeared at Tairseach all the time, even though it was abandoned by the druids long ago. And she'd often say . . ." he trailed off, seeming reluctant to continue. "She'd say that these people were coming from and going to other times."

Ciaran stiffened, astonishment flooding him.

"Other times? As in—past and future?"

"Aye. Given Isabelle's odd manner of speech, and Donella mentioning that she wore strange underclothes, a part of me has wondered . . ."

Gabhran flushed as he trailed off, a look of embar-rassment flashing across his face.

Ciaran's heart hammered as he stared at Gabhran. Isabelle's words rang in his mind: *I know this is going to sound crazy, but I'm not from this time.*

"I ken 'tis nonsense, there's no need tae look at me like that," Gabhran grumbled.

"'Tis not strange—we all have our supersti-tions," Ciaran forced himself to say, his gut filling with turmoil. Could Isabelle be speaking the truth? Was the lass from the future?

"I ken. Forget I said anything of it. And doonae tell Donella, she would laugh at such foolishness," Gabhran said.

Before Ciaran could answer, there was a sharp knock at the door, and relief flooded him. He didn't want to dwell on Tairseach and the notion of a person traveling through time.

Gabhran opened the door to reveal three men standing there. He waved them in with a wide smile.

"These are my most loyal men," Gabhran said. "Wylie, Somerled, and Ranulf. They've agreed tae help ye."

"I thank ye," Ciaran said, facing them. "I'll need ye tae return tae Aitharne Castle where ye can pose as stable workers—the stables are always in need of men. Find my friend Lachaid; he'll help ye and can be trusted. Focus on anyone who seems at odds with my brother—they're the ones most likely tae help us. If ye suspect ye're in danger or at risk of being found out, get yerself out of there. Even if ye doonae have the information ye need. I'll not have any man die for me. Understood?"

The men slid their gazes to Gabhran before nodding their agreement.

"Report back tae us after a week," Gabhran added.

When Gabhran's men left the study, Ciaran watched them go with a thundering heart. He hated that there wasn't more he could do. He was usually the one in charge, but now he felt helpless.

"We'll get him," Gabhran said, resting his hand on Ciaran's shoulder. "We'll bring yer brother tae justice. And then ye'll have yer life back."

CHAPTER 12

The day after their kiss, Isabelle realized that Ciaran seemed determined to pretend she didn't exist—and that the kiss never happened.

At breakfast, he avoided looking at her, though she caught him staring at her with those hypnotic hazel eyes at least twice. He then holed up with Gabhran in his study.

Once they were alone, Donella offered to take her on a tour of the manor and its expansive grounds. Needing a distraction, Isabelle agreed.

As they walked, Donella told Isabelle how she and Gabhran met. She was the daughter of a merchant from Edinburgh who moved to the Highlands to settle in with their clan. Her marriage to Gabhran wasn't arranged; he'd pursued and married her out of love.

"'Tis a large home for just the three of us and our servants," Donella said, as she led Isabelle down the main corridor of the manor. "I hope God sees fit I have more bairns to fill it with. Gabhran's a wonderful father. I never saw my father growing up, but Gabhran takes great pains tae spend time with Annis."

Donella cocked her head to the side, studying Isabelle.

"Where in England did ye say ye're from? Ye have quite a strange accent."

Isabelle's heart picked up its pace, and she swallowed.

"Just a small village in the south of England. I doubt you've heard of it," she said. "I live with my brother; I miss him a great deal," she added, deciding to stick as close to the truth as possible. "He knows I'm here searching for Fiona. I don't know where she is in the Highlands, but I hope to find her."

Donella's expression softened with sympathy.

"If our messenger doesnae find her in the village, I can have him search others nearby."

"Thank you," Isabelle said with a grateful smile. She liked Donella and hated that she had to lie about her backstory, but it was a necessary evil.

"I ken 'tis none of my concern, but ye and Ciaran seem tae be keeping yer distance from each other," Donella said. "I find it odd, given how much he looks at ye when he thinks ye doonae notice."

Isabelle flushed, trying to keep her expression neutral.

"Ciaran and I are just . . . acquaintances. I'm

grateful to him for his rescue and escort, but that's all there is to our relationship," Isabelle said, not able to look Donella in the eye. *An acquaintance I've kissed. An acquaintance I'm wildly attracted to.*

"Then I'll not meddle," Donella said, though Isabelle could tell by her discerning look that she didn't believe her. "But I will say he seems taken with ye, and I've never seen Ciaran taken with anyone."

In spite of herself, hope filled Isabelle at Donella's words. But when they sat down to supper with Gabhran and Ciaran, Ciaran still avoided looking at her. She had to force a polite smile as she engaged in light chatter with Donella and Gabhran.

When she retired to her chamber, she leaned back against the door, an ache gnawing at her over Ciaran's avoidance. She reached up to touch her lips, closing her eyes. Had it only been last night that they'd shared such a passionate, soul-shattering kiss? She'd barely been able to walk straight after it. *If he kisses like that,* a voice whispered, *what would his lovemaking be like?*

The images came to her unbidden. Ciaran's muscled body lowering her to the bed, his lips on every part of her body, the long hard length of him sinking into her. Moisture crept between her thighs, and Isabelle swallowed, forcing the erotic images from her mind.

What the hell was wrong with her? She had

traveled back six hundred years in time not to salivate over a hunky Scot, but to find her best friend.

Donella and Gabhran had kept to their word, sending a messenger to the nearest village to inquire about a Fiona Stewart, a lass with a strange accent about her age, but so far there had been no word.

But what else could she expect? In the present, an internet search could find just about anyone. Finding Fiona in this time was indeed like searching for a needle in a haystack. All she could do for now was rely on Gabhran and Donella's messenger for news, and push aside the fear that she'd never find Fiona, that she'd have to return to her own time with a lingering question mark over Fiona's fate.

You will find her, she assured herself, as she undressed and slipped into bed. But to her shame, it wasn't Fiona she thought of as she drifted off to sleep. It was Ciaran.

A ROUTINE of sorts developed over the next couple of days. Isabelle would share a morning meal with Donella. Sometimes Gabhran and Ciaran would join them, with Ciaran continuing his habit of not looking at her, before they would retire to their study, where Donella told her they were working together with Gabhran's men to find ways of clearing his name.

Isabelle and Donella would then spend the morning with Gabhran and Donella's daughter Annis. At eight years old, she was more precocious than the jaded teenaged students Isabelle taught in the twenty-first century. Isabelle would sit with Annis as Donella taught her embroidery or told Annis stories before they shared a midday meal. Isabelle would then take long walks around the gardens before having supper with them.

Gabhran and Donella's messenger kept returning with no news of Fiona, and Isabelle's hopes of finding her friend began to decrease. There would be no use remaining here if she made no progress in finding her.

Isabelle was mulling over this one afternoon as she strolled through the back gardens. For some reason, a part of her resisted leaving quite yet, and her thoughts strayed to Ciaran. Surely she wasn't lingering here because of him?

She yelped when she almost collided with a broad, muscular torso. She looked up, startled. It was Ciaran.

She'd almost forgotten the physical effect he had on her. As his hazel eyes probed hers, her throat went dry and her pulse fluttered wildly beneath her skin, as rapid as a hummingbird's wings. It didn't help that he looked particularly gorgeous today, in a dark tunic and belted green plaid kilt, his dark hair ruffled, as if he'd run his hands through it many times. Her gaze dropped to his sensual lips, recalling the feel of them pressed to hers, and a surge of lust flowed through her.

"May I join ye, lass?" he asked, his voice husky. "On yer walk?"

"But—you've been avoiding me," she blurted, her eyes widening with surprise.

"Aye," he said, with an apologetic smile. "I felt guilty for kissing ye. I'm an outlaw, Isabelle. I doonae want tae put ye in any danger."

"And you want to walk with me now?" she challenged.

"Aye," he murmured, taking a step closer to her, and her heart rate skyrocketed. "I find I cannae stay away from ye, lass. I—I watch ye," he admitted, pointing up to a window on the second floor. "Every day that ye walk."

Isabelle stilled. She'd felt eyes on her during her walks; she'd assumed it was the curious servants. But it was Ciaran who'd been watching her. An unexpected ripple of delight filled her at the thought.

"I suppose you can join me," she said, giving him a light smile.

Ciaran's shoulders sank with relief; he must have thought she'd refuse him. They began to walk among the fragrant flowers of the garden, which Donella told her was surprisingly fertile for the Highlands. But Isabelle paid no attention to her surroundings, only aware of Ciaran's presence at her side. She was always only aware of his presence when he was near.

"Is there any progress?" she asked tentatively. "With clearing your name?"

"No," Ciaran said, his eyes darkening. "Not yet. It will take some time, but I confess I'm not the most patient man."

His eyes swept to the flowers that filled the gardens.

"This reminds me of the gardens my mother had planted at the castle before she died. My father entrusted me and my brothers with its upkeep." His face shadowed at the mention of his brothers.

"Is this manor anything like your castle?" she asked, hoping she could help take his focus off of Tavish and Eoin.

"No," he said, his expression softening with a look of nostalgia. "My castle isnae on open land. 'Tis surrounded by trees and a wee loch nearby. 'Tis said my ancestors built the castle there for solitude, a closeness tae nature. I've never kent another home. Nor would I want tae."

Pain flared in his eyes, and Isabelle reached out to place a comforting hand on his arm. He stiffened, and she started to remove her hand.

"No, lass," he said, reaching out to keep her hand on his arm. He looked at her, his eyes twinkling with mischief. "I enjoy yer touch more than ye realize."

Isabelle smiled, flushing as he tucked her hand into the crook of his arm.

"And ye? What's yer home like?"

She gave him a wary look. "I've told you where I'm from. You don't believe me."

An odd look filled Ciaran's eyes before he averted his gaze.

"I believe ye have a home," he said quietly.

"Well, I live in a large city," she hedged, as Chicago didn't exist in this time.

"Like Edinburgh? London?"

"Yes," she said, deciding to keep her descriptions vague and avoid mentioning things such as technology, skyscrapers, or cars. "My home—my apartment—is the size of my guest chamber," she continued, thinking of her small apartment in the north side of Chicago.

"The size of a chamber? Yer entire home?" Ciaran asked, looking surprised and mildly horrified.

Isabelle shook her head and chuckled. Ciaran and his friends, as kind as they were, were the aristocratic class of this time. She was speaking to a man who'd grown up in a castle surrounded by servants.

"Not everyone can live in castles or manors," she said with a teasing smile. "I can only afford a 'chamber'. Teachers don't make much where I'm from." *When I'm from,* she silently added.

"My tutors were some of the best paid men in my clan," Ciaran said, frowning down at her. "But none of them are lasses."

"Where I'm from, there are plenty of 'lass'

teachers," Isabelle said, leveling him with a hard stare, as if daring him to challenge her.

But he didn't. Instead, he laughed. Ciaran laughed with his whole body; he threw his head back and his broad shoulders shook. Isabelle couldn't help but smile at the sight.

"I believe ye, lass. And I believe ye're a good tutor. Ye mentioned a brother. Is he a tutor as well?"

Isabelle stilled, her heart tightening at the thought of her brother. *Scott.* He must be worried sick about her.

"Yes," she murmured. "He teaches classic literature; it's something we share a love for. He's the only family member I'm close to. It's just the two of us; our parents died years ago."

"I'm sorry about yer parents," Ciaran murmured. "I think of my own parents often."

Grief flared in his eyes, and Isabelle squeezed his hand as they continued to walk in companionable silence.

After that first walk, Ciaran joined her on a daily basis, and she looked forward to their walks. Donella and Gabhran seemed pleased by her and Ciaran's growing closeness, often leaving them alone on purpose with knowing smiles.

During their walks, Isabelle learned more about Ciaran and his life before everything turned upside down. His father had made him laird and chief of his clan after he'd passed, and his duties had consumed his life. The only leisure he'd had time for was hunting trips with his brother Eoin, who often encouraged him to take breaks and live more of his life outside of the constraints of his duties.

As for her own life, Isabelle was hesitant to tell him more about her, given that he didn't believe she was from the future.

"Ye can tell me," Ciaran insisted. "I'll listen without judgment. Ye have my word."

And so she told him about her job and how much she enjoyed teaching English, details of her relationship with Scott, and how close she and Fiona had been—and how much she missed her. He kept to his word and listened with genuine interest, with no skepticism, and she wondered if he was slowly starting to believe her.

While they walked, he would tuck her hand into the crook of his arm but made no other attempts to touch or kiss her—to her great disappointment.

Yet as much as she desired him, she began to appreciate and crave more things about him than just his stunningly good looks. He had a sizable sense of humor, and did impressions of Gabhran when he was a wild and carefree young man that made her laugh. He had a sense of honor that didn't exist in her own time, and given his grief and guilt over Eoin's murder, she could tell he was deeply loyal to those he loved.

While Isabelle cherished her time with Ciaran, in the back of her mind she reminded herself that this was all temporary. Their time together was brief, a shining momentary suspension of time before she returned to the twenty-first century.

She didn't allow herself to dwell too much on this, but whenever she did, the grief that seized her signaled that her feelings for Ciaran had grown much deeper than she'd thought.

Ciaran could no longer deny it to himself. He craved the lass. And not just her body, though images of her curves filled his dreams at night. He craved the sound of her laughter, which reminded him of tinkling bells, her smile, which shone with incandescence and filled him with joy of his own, even the gentle hum of her voice.

And given what Gabhran had told him about Tairseach, he couldn't believe that the kind and thoughtful lass he was coming to know would tell him such an elaborate lie. But his lingering uncertainty about the notion of a person traveling through time was in constant battle with his tentative belief in her tale. He decided to ignore his inner turmoil, instead choosing to focus on the pleasure of her company.

He continued to receive periodic updates from Gabhran about his men; they were in place at his castle and in contact with Lachaid, but they'd learned nothing of use.

"I ken 'tis hard," Gabhran told him. "But 'tis best we wait till they uncover something. My men are good. Have faith, Ciaran. They will find something that can help."

It was hard putting his complete trust into others to help him, but he tried to abide by Gabhran's words.

And while he could have patience for updates from Gabhran's men, he could no longer practice patience when it came to his desire for Isabelle.

He thought their daily walks would satisfy him, but it wasn't enough. He desired Isabelle with a ferocity that seized every part of him. He needed more. And he suspected she felt the same, by the way her eyes sometimes lingered on his lips, or how her gaze trailed up and down his body.

They'd been at the manor for over a fortnight when he asked her to take a walk with him after dinner. He saw the surprise that flared in her lovely eyes when he didn't lead her out to the garden, but to her guest chamber.

"Isabelle," he whispered. "Ye must ken by now that I want ye. But I'll not bring dishonor tae ye if ye doonae feel the same."

He waited for her response, his heart thundering in his ears. Isabelle lowered her eyes, and he feared she would refuse him. But she stood on her tiptoes, pressing her lips to his.

"Please," she murmured. "Dishonor me, Ciaran."

He let out a strangled moan at the seductive invitation in her voice, and swung her up into his arms. Isabelle laughed with surprise and delight as he stepped into her chamber, kicking the door shut behind them. He carried her to the bed as she lowered her hand to the hardness that swelled beneath his kilt, stroking him.

"Christ, lass," he moaned, lowering her to the bed and stripping her of her clothing with such roughness he feared he would tear her fine gown. But there was no quelling the desire that rushed through him with the force of a raging river. He could no longer contain himself around her.

Isabelle helped him undress, her breathing ragged as she stripped him of his tunic and kilt.

"Ciaran," she whispered, pressing her hands to his muscular abdomen, leaning forward to place kisses along the expanse of his torso. The feel of her lips against his skin filled him with an ache, and he groaned, capturing her hands with his and lowering her back to the bed.

"No, lass," he said gently, surveying the lovely curves of her body before leaning down to capture her lips with his own. "I need tae touch ye first."

He kissed her slowly, leisurely, until she was whimpering beneath him, before dragging his lips down to the flesh of her throat, where he nibbled at the soft skin there. He continued to pepper kisses down to her breasts, looking up to meet her eyes as he captured one nipple in his mouth, suckling at it until she threw her head back and moaned.

He seized her other nipple with his mouth, kneading the free breast with his hand, relishing in the feel of it in his hand as he suckled.

Isabelle's body quivered when he released her breasts from his hands and mouth. He kissed down her abdomen to the tops of her thighs where he wedged her legs open with his broad shoulders.

He looked up as her blue eyes locked with his, hazy with desire. He kept his eyes trained on hers as he kissed the inside of her left thigh, then her right, before clamping his mouth onto her sweet center.

"Oh, God," Isabelle cried as he tasted her, his tongue delving into her sweetness. She began to writhe, and he reached up to grip her breasts as he continued to feast, moaning out his pleasure at the taste of her on his tongue.

He could have feasted on her forever, but his own hardness was becoming painful, and he reached down to stroke himself as Isabelle's release claimed her. She cried out as her orgasm tore through her, spilling her delectable juices into his mouth. He continued to lick her sweetness as her quivering slowed and came to a stop before reluctantly lifting his head.

"Ciaran," she said on a moan, her eyes closed. "Please . . ."

"I ken, lass," he whispered, lifting himself above her, taking in the beauty of her nude form. "Look at me," he ordered, with a sudden possessiveness that surprised him. He needed her to know exactly who was claiming her, who was giving her pleasure.

She opened her eyes, training them on him, and the heady desire in them was so stark that he let out a pleasured groan as he sank his cock into her.

Isabelle gasped, throwing her head back in ecstasy. Ciaran held himself still, allowing her to adjust to his size, but it was difficult—she felt like heaven clenched around him, and he wanted nothing more than to thrust her beautiful body into the bed with the force of his desire.

Finally, he began to move, slow and steady, letting out a groan between clenched teeth. Isabelle whimpered, wrapping her legs around him to pull him deeper inside her. He lost control then, increasing the force of his thrusts until he was pounding her into the bed. He suckled at her throat as they moved together, then her lips, then her breasts, unable to keep himself from tasting her as he claimed her in the most intimate way.

He didn't know how long they moved together, the bed shaking beneath them as he thrust into her, but soon sweat soaked their heated bodies, and he could feel the force of his release start to spiral deep within his belly. But he wanted to wait; he could tell from Isabelle's moans and trembling form that she was close to another release. So he held back, gritting his teeth with effort as he continued to pound her into the bed.

"Come for me, Isabelle," he whispered. "Come for me, my beauty."

"Ciaran," she gasped. "Oh, God—Ciaran!"

She reached up to grip his shoulders as her release claimed her, her body trembling beneath him, her breath coming in shuddering gasps. Ciaran could no longer hold his own release at bay. He reached down to hold her body close to his as his orgasm claimed him, and he came with a ragged cry, burying his face in her neck as he spilled his cum inside her.

They remained locked together for several moments, their ragged breathing the only sound in the room, until he reluctantly disengaged himself from Isabelle's body. But he continued to hold her close, reaching out to stroke the damp strands of her hair back from her face.

"I cannae get enough of ye, lass," he whispered. "Do ye have any notion of how desirable ye are?"

Isabelle flushed in response, giving him a shy smile.

"I've wanted you ever since I saw you washing in that stream," she confessed.

"Aye?" he asked with a grin. "Well, I was thinking of ye as I washed, all dirty and frightened in those man's clothes ye were wearing. Had ye come a moment later, ye may have seen me stroking myself."

Isabelle's eyes widened in surprise, and her flush deepened.

"I've wanted ye since I first saw ye, Isabelle," he

continued. "I was so entangled in my troubles . . . and then ye came intae my life. Now ye're all I can think about. All I desire."

Isabelle leaned forward to press a kiss to his lips. But her smile faded as she studied him.

"What?"

"You want me . . . even though you think I'm lying to you? About being from the future?"

"I doonae think ye're lying tae me," he said, after a brief pause. "But ye must understand . . . 'tis hard tae believe. I doonae ken how 'tis possible."

"Neither do I," Isabelle said, shaking her head with frustration. "But it is, because I'm here."

He studied her desperate and imploring expression, recalling the strange clothes she wore when he first met her, her odd manner of speech. Her asking him what year it was when they'd first met. The truth in her words when she spoke about her life before she'd stumbled across him in that forest. And Gabhran's story about Tairseach, which had lingered in the back of his mind.

She wasn't like any lass he'd ever met. As impossible as it was . . . it made sense that she was from another time.

Perhaps he'd known deep down she was telling the truth. Perhaps he'd held onto his denial because he knew that if she was from another time . . . she would one day return to it.

"I believe ye, lass," he murmured, though his heart tightened at the realization that she didn't belong here.

CHAPTER 14

The look of relief that crossed her expression was so stark that Ciaran felt guilty for not believing her sooner.

"You believe me?" she whispered. "Really?"

"Aye," he confirmed. "I doonae understand it . . . but I believe ye."

He told her about Gabhran's tale of Tairseach, and his initial suspicion of Isabelle. She sat up at this, her eyes going wide.

"He has no idea how right he is," she murmured. "I've caught him studying me a couple of times . . . now I know why."

"I trust Gabhran with my life," he said gravely. "But 'tis best we keep this tae ourselves. Many in the Highlands are superstitious, and a Sassenach rumored tae come from the future will encourage whispers of witchcraft."

Isabelle paled and swallowed hard.

"All right," she said. "Let's keep this to ourselves."

"How did it happen?" he asked, wanting to change the subject, to wipe that look of fear from her expression. "When ye traveled through time?"

Ciaran listened intently as Isabelle told him of a woman named Kensa who took her to Tairseach, the tug of wind that yanked her backward, and Kensa's cryptic words about her not belonging in her own time.

"Have you ever fallen down from a great height?" Isabelle asked.

"I fell from my horse once," he said. "Broke my leg."

"Imagine falling from the height of . . . fifty horses," Isabelle said. "Only at a rapid speed and surrounded by darkness. That's how it felt. And when I came to, I was in that muddy stream. I think . . . I think Fiona may have also traveled through time, that Kensa did the same thing to her."

"Ye will find yer friend," Ciaran assured her, taking in the look of worry on her face. "It may take time, but I can tell how determined ye are."

"I hope so," Isabelle whispered.

After a brief pause, Ciaran reached out to stroke the silken strands of her hair. She leaned in to his touch, resting her head on his chest.

"What is this future like?" Ciaran asked, continuing to stroke her hair.

Isabelle told him of buildings as high as mountains, carriages powered by things called engines and not horses, small objects called phones that worked like letters, connecting people across great distances. She told him about social changes; women attending university and holding jobs of their own like she did.

He found this all strange and fascinating, but he wanted to know more about her in this future.

"Ye told me ye taught English? At this school of high?" he asked.

"High school," Isabelle corrected, her lips twitching in a smile. "And, yes. But many young people in my time aren't very interested in old books and classics. Every once in awhile, I'll get a student who's as excited about classics as I am."

"What's yer favorite of these?" he asked. "These classics?"

"Many of the Greek ones, especially the myths. The one about Orpheus descending to—"

"Tae hell. To rescue the woman he loves," he finished for her. At the surprise that flared in her eyes, he gave her a teasing grin. "What? Ye doonae believe a Highlander can read the classics? I told ye my castle had fine tutors. 'Tis one of my favorite tales."

"Really?" she asked, looking at him with the eagerness of a wee lass, and he chuckled.

"Aye," he said. "Ye'd have liked Eoin. He also liked reading, telling tales. He . . ." Ciaran trailed off as an image of his brother's kind face filled his mind. He wasn't prepared for the sudden grief that gripped him. He closed his eyes against a sting of tears.

"Ciaran."

He opened his eyes. Isabelle had taken his hand, her expression filled with warmth and empathy.

"Don't fight your grief. Pushing it away only makes it worse. Allow yourself to grieve. It's the only way to move forward."

He wanted to resist her words, to return to the numbness he'd given into ever since his arrest for Eoin's murder. But Isabelle had already changed something in him . . . she'd splintered the walls he'd erected around his heart.

"It's all right," Isabelle murmured. She reached out to pull him close, and Ciaran buried his face in the crook of her neck, his sweet Isabelle, and he wept.

As THE EARLY morning light of dawn filtered into Isabelle's chamber, they awoke at the same time, and Ciaran made love to her again. This time it was less fervent, but all the more passionate, his eyes locked on hers as he moved within her, their inti-mate movements hushed and unhurried in the silence of first light.

"Tell me more about him," Isabelle whispered afterward, as they held each other. "Your brother."

He told her all about Eoin, how he always

found the joy in everyday living, how well-liked he was among the clan, how he was able to make even the sternest noble laugh.

"I tried tae have the same bond with Tavish that I had with Eoin. But he remained cold and closed off—he's been that way since he was a bairn. I'd no idea he hated me so. I should have kent."

"You couldn't have," Isabelle said firmly. "And all that's in the past. What matters now is how you move forward."

Her words settled in, and a renewed surge of determination flowed through him. If Gabhran's men weren't finding anything, he would have to try something else. Perhaps even find another clan to ally with him. He couldn't let Tavish get away with what he'd done.

Ciaran stilled as the sound of multiple horse hooves splintered the silence.

He scrambled out of bed. Shock skittered through him when he looked out the window. Several men on horseback approached the manor. As they drew closer, he recognized his brother as one of them.

Tavish had found him.

CHAPTER 15

*I*sabelle got out of bed, clutching the sheets around her nude body, her chest growing tight. Ciaran's face had gone white as he stared out the window.

"What is it?" she whispered.

"'Tis my brother. And his men," he said grimly, turning to face her.

"Oh my God," Isabelle gasped. She stood frozen as Ciaran moved to the foot of the bed and scooped his clothing off the floor.

"Ye're tae stay in this chamber," he ordered, not looking at her as he got dressed. "If I turn myself in now, they'll have no reason tae come inside the manor."

Horror flooded Isabelle's body as she hastily got dressed.

"Turn yourself in?"

"Aye. I'll not have ye nor my friends harmed because of my presence here."

"No," Isabelle protested, reaching out to grip his arm. "Tavish will have you hanged if you return."

"'Tis not yer concern," Ciaran said, gently removing her hand. "Get yerself back to Tairseach —back tae yer own time once I'm gone."

Panic coursed through Isabelle, and she shook her head. She couldn't just leave Ciaran to be executed. An overwhelming sense of grief swept over her at the thought.

She took several deep breaths, willing herself to calm, to think. And then an idea struck her.

"Ciaran, wait. Please. I have an idea."

"Isabelle—"

"Think of Eoin," she interrupted. "Didn't you say you wanted to avenge him? Are you just going to give up?"

"Tavish is here. There's no time tae plan a—"

"Please just hear me out. My idea can give you more time."

His expression remained tense, but he expelled a wary sigh.

"All right, lass. What's yer plan?"

MOMENTS LATER, Isabelle stood outside the drawing room, her heart hammering erratically in her chest. Inside, Tavish and two of his men stood opposite Gabhran and Donella, grilling them about Ciaran's whereabouts. She'd only had moments to tell them her plan; to her relief they'd agreed to play along, as desperate to save Ciaran as she was.

Isabelle took several deep breaths before pushing open the door. It was showtime.

Gabhran turned, his eyes widening at the sight of her. His acting skills impressed her, as he stood and bellowed, "Isabelle! I told ye tae stay in yer chamber."

Tavish and his men turned to face her. She tried not to flinch at Tavish's hard gaze. Unlike his brother, he was fair with blond hair and blue eyes, and unlike Ciaran's natural warmth, there was a frostiness to him she could sense from several feet away.

"I—I'm sorry," she said, hoping that she looked both startled and bashful. Tavish's eyes narrowed at the sound of her odd accent. She turned as if to leave, but Tavish crossed the room to her in several large strides.

"And just who are ye, lass?" he growled.

"A guest," Gabhran said. "She has nothing tae—"

"The lass can speak for herself," Tavish interjected, his eyes trained on hers. "I'll only ask once more. Who are ye, lass?"

She looked at him with fear, which she didn't have to feign. Tavish's coldness was intimidating.

"I—I'm from England and was traveling through these parts to visit a cousin. Bandits overtook my coach. I—"

"The lass has spoken enough," Gabhran interrupted. "Isabelle, leave here now."

"If ye doonae silence yerself Gabhran, I'll have my men do it for ye," Tavish snapped. "Finish yer story, lass."

Isabelle swallowed. This next part was a crucial part of her plan; she needed to sell it.

"A man rescued me when the bandits attacked. Told me his name was Ciaran. He left me here so I could arrange transport and continue on my way, and—"

"Stop it, Isabelle!" Gabhran shouted. "Keep yer mouth—"

One of Tavish's men took a menacing step toward Gabhran, and Donella rushed to his side. Isabelle stilled, clenching her hands at her sides. She didn't want to risk Tavish's men hurting Gabhran, but the look in his eyes urged her to continue.

"Continue, lass," Tavish ordered.

"Ciaran told us that he didn't want to put his friends in danger, so he was going to stay with a trusted friend in Edinburgh."

Gabhran and Donella looked at her in horror, and their performance again pleased her. She turned her gaze back to Tavish, the person who needed to buy their performance the most.

A look of dark pleasure filled his eyes and revulsion roiled through her. How could the handsome and honorable Ciaran be related by blood to this snake? But she kept the expression of frightened confusion on her face.

"Ye did good, lass," he murmured. "I ken several possible men he'll seek out in Edinburgh. I doonae ken why Gabhran wants tae protect a murderer and traitor."

His expression turned lascivious as his eyes trailed down to the curve of her breasts beneath her bodice.

"Perhaps I can help ye get back tae England on our way tae Edinburgh?"

"That is very kind of you," Isabelle forced herself to say, though disgust filled her at the thought of going anywhere with this man. "But transport has already been arranged for me."

"If Gabhran wasnae hosting such a bonnie lass and showing her hospitality—and if it wouldnae start a clan war—I'd have him hanged for treason and his wife and daughter sent tae a nunnery," he said coldly, shooting Gabhran a glare over his shoulder. "But I must continue the hunt for my treacherous brother. I thank ye for yer honesty, lass."

He reached out to take her hand, lifting it to his lips for a kiss. Another wave of revulsion roiled through her, but she made herself smile.

"If only we'd met under different circumstances, lass," he murmured, his eyes darkening with desire.

"We need tae be on our way, m'laird," one of his men interrupted, to Isabelle's immense relief. "This weather willnae hold. Our horses cannae ride fast if the rain is heavy."

Tavish nodded, but his gaze lingered on hers. Isabelle swallowed, fearing he'd insist she come with them. But he turned, gesturing for his men to follow him out.

She moved to stand next to Gabhran and Donella as they watched Tavish and his men ride away from the manor. It was only when they disappeared into the distance that Isabelle's shoulders sank with relief.

It worked, she thought in a daze. Her plan had worked, and she'd bought Ciaran time.

Ciaran entered the room once Tavish and his men were out of sight, and she rushed to him, burying her face in the crook of his neck as he held her close.

"I'm glad ye're safe," he whispered, stroking her hair. "It took everything in me not tae charge in here when he touched ye."

She pulled back, looking up at him with horror.

"You were watching? Ciaran, you were supposed to be hiding in the stables!"

During her hastily put-together plan, they'd decided that Ciaran would stay out of sight in the stables while they put on their performance. Dread filled her at the thought of what would've happened if Tavish had spotted him.

"I couldnae risk him hurting any of ye on account of me," Ciaran said. "I was in the next room over, they didnae see me."

"Isabelle did well. Yer brother believed her," Donella said with a smile.

"Thanks," Isabelle said, returning her smile. "So did the both of you."

"I cannae stay here," Ciaran interjected, and Isabelle's relief dissipated. "Tavish coming here only proves how dangerous it is for me tae be here."

"No, Ciaran," Gabhran protested. "We sent him away."

"My brother will discover I'm not in Edinburgh; he'll return here. And when he returns, he'll not show ye any mercy. I need tae get more men on my side before he comes back—and not just for me, but tae protect all of ye. May I talk tae Isabelle alone?" he added abruptly, and Isabelle stiffened with dread.

After Gabhran and Donella obliged and left them alone, Ciaran took her hand, turning her to face him.

"Ye need tae go on yer way. When Tavish realizes ye lied tae him, that ye're helping me . . . " he trailed off, his face draining of color. "I've seen how he treats lasses who displease him. Ye must get back tae yer time, Isabelle."

Isabelle stilled, pain spiraling in her chest.

"But, Fiona—" she began.

"I assume yer friend would want ye tae be safe," he interrupted. "I can give her name tae people I ken, arrange for word tae get tae ye if she's found. Gabhran and Donella will also keep up the search."

"What about you?" Isabelle pressed "Where are you going to go?"

"There's a high-ranking noble I ken—Artair Brothaig. I doonae ken the man very well, but he was an ally of my father's once and may help. Gabhran told me he resides not far from Tairseach. I'll take ye tae Tairseach, then seek refuge with him."

Uncertainty filled Isabelle's gut, and she opened her mouth to protest. But he placed his thumb over her lip to silence her, regret flaring in his hazel eyes.

"I wish we'd met a different way, lass," he murmured. It was an echo of his brother's words, but Ciaran's words filled her with painful longing. Not only had they met under the wrong circumstances—they'd met at the wrong time.

He leaned down to place a brief kiss on her lips before leaving her alone in the drawing room. She stood there for several moments, her eyes closed, pressing her fingers to her lips where he'd kissed her, as if she could sear the memory of his kiss onto them.

Isabelle kept to her chamber for the rest of the day, declining even to eat with the others. She told herself that Ciaran was right; it was too dangerous for her here and Fiona would want her to be safe. Besides, she now had people who would keep up the search after she was back in the twenty-first century. She just needed to make sure they got a letter to her the way Fiona had if they found her.

Yet her self-talk did nothing to assuage the anguish that filled her over the prospect of her looming separation from Ciaran. And there was something else lingering beneath her sadness, an unease she couldn't quite understand.

It wasn't until she was preparing for bed that the cause of her unease struck her. It was the noble Ciaran mentioned. *Artair*.

Isabelle fled from her chamber, racing down the hall to find Ciaran. The entire time she'd been in the fourteenth century, her knowledge of the future had done nothing to help present events.

Until now.

CHAPTER 16

*C*iaran stiffened as Isabelle entered his chamber, a heated awareness rippling through him at the sight of her in her underdress. It clung to her curves, and he ached to pull her into his arms, to carry her to his bed and bury himself inside her.

And had it not been for his brother's visit, he would have.

He'd had a taste of her for one night, and he'd have to be satisfied with that. Fear gripped him at the thought of Tavish capturing her, of taking his revenge for helping him. To keep her safe, he'd have to put his longing for her aside.

Ciaran straightened, holding himself rigid as she approached, not letting his gaze slip to the outline of her breasts beneath her dress.

"Ye shouldnae be in here, lass."

"I know," she said. "But I needed to warn you

about that noble you mentioned, Artair. You can't trust him."

"How do ye ken?"

"I've heard of him in my time. Remember Kensa, the woman I told you about? She told me about him, and I don't think it's a coincidence that she did. Two years from now, he'll be hung for betraying several clans—working behind their backs to turn them against each other and profiting from their conflicts. If you go to him, I have no doubt he'll go to Tavish and turn you in."

Ciaran went still, considering her words. He didn't know Artair well, but there were rampant rumors about his mercenary nature. Yet Ciaran had limited options when it came to his choice of allies.

"I thank ye," he said, expelling a heavy sigh. He'd have to make alternative plans, though it would prove difficult to find men not allied with Clan Aitharne who'd take him in.

"What are you going to do?"

"'Tis not yer concern. Soon," his voice wavered, but he forced himself to continue, "soon, ye'll be back in yer own time, far from my troubles."

Isabelle bit her lip, her lovely eyes filling with tears.

"I doonae want tae send ye away," he whispered. "But ye understand how dangerous it is for ye here, aye?"

"I do," Isabelle said. "But I also don't want anything to happen to you. I . . . I care about you, Ciaran. You don't deserve this. Any of it."

"Doonae fret. I've other allies in the Highlands. It may be more difficult tae get tae them, but I will."

He reached down to wipe away a stray tear on her face with his thumb. Isabelle stilled at his touch; he heard her breath catch in her throat as her eyes lifted to his.

Ciaran's gaze lowered to her mouth, to the curve of her shoulders, to her breasts. He should tell her to return to her chamber. But his body wouldn't listen. His heart wouldn't.

He pulled her into the circle of his arms, pressing his lips to hers. The heat that filled him flared to a simmering inferno, and his cock stirred beneath his kilt.

"Ciaran," Isabelle breathed against his mouth, "if we're to have one last night together . . . then let's make it count."

She stepped back, and his mouth went dry as she lowered her underdress to stand nude before him.

He growled at her challenge, moving forward to again capture her mouth with his. His desire was so great that he didn't have the patience to get to the bed; he sank to his knees before her, gripping her buttocks and pulling her sweet quim to his mouth.

"Oh my God," she gasped, her hands going to his hair, pressing him more firmly against her. He continued to lick and probe her center, needing to remember her taste, to sear it into his memory. He didn't stop until she quaked her release, and he lowered her to the floor.

"I'm sorry," he groaned. "I cannae wait any longer."

Isabelle gasped as he stripped off his clothing and sank his hard length inside her. She wound her arms around his neck, her breath coming out in gasps as he began to thrust. Their eyes locked as he pounded into her, and he leaned down to plunder her mouth with his tongue. It wasn't long before he felt the stirrings of his release tug on him, and he came with a roar, holding her close as her body shook with her own release.

They were both still breathless as he sat up, gently scooping her into his arms. He carried her to the bed, his eyes trailing down the loveliness of her nude body—her full breasts, the flat plane of her abdomen, the gentle swell of her hips—and he hardened once more.

Isabelle's eyes widened at the sight of his erection, and he gave her a mischievous grin.

"Ye said tae make this night count, my bonnie Isabelle," he whispered, crawling on top of her, hissing at the feel of her naked flesh against his. "I intend tae make it so."

CIARAN AWOKE LONG before Isabelle the next morning, his dread like a great weight in his heart. After he'd made love to her the second time, they'd spend the night talking, avoiding the subject of their looming separation. Instead, they spoke of the classics he and Isabelle were both fond of, the precociousness of Gabhran and Donella's daughter, his friendship with Gabhran, which she told him seemed akin to her friendship with Fiona. He'd remained awake after she'd fallen asleep, gazing down at her, wanting to remember every detail of this bonnie time traveler who'd entered his life and filled it with momentary joy.

Today he would return her to Tairseach and they would part ways. She would be off to her own time, a future in which he didn't exist. He looked down at her sleeping form, a dark resentment crawling through him, resentment of this future that would have his Isabelle. She was too bonnie to stay alone for long; one day a man would claim her heart and body for his own.

He closed his eyes, allowing himself to imagine a different future for them. He imagined her as lady of Aitharne Castle. Spending the days with her reading and discussing the classics she was so fond of. Spending the nights with her body entwined with his.

But it was not to be. His brother wouldn't stop until he had Ciaran hanging from a noose. And while that was true, everyone he cared for was in danger.

Isabelle was quiet when she came to and got dressed. He'd thought she would be glad to return to her own time, but her expression was shadowed.

She barely spoke as they shared a brief meal with Gabhran and Donella, and her silence lingered even as they embraced them farewell.

"Stay safe," Ciaran said, gripping Gabhran's shoulders, as they stood in front of the manor. "Take yer family and go into hiding if my brother comes back."

"I ken how tae handle yer brother," Gabhran replied with a scowl. "Ye think ye'll be safe with this other clan?"

Ciaran nodded, though he wasn't certain. He planned to head north, to seek refuge with a small clan who had always been friendly to him. He prayed they would take him in.

Gabhran glanced over at Isabelle, who walked to their horse with Donella. "Are ye sure ye want tae part ways with the lass?"

"I've no choice," Ciaran said, pain splintering his heart at the words. "She's not from these parts, 'tis not her fight. 'Tis best for her tae return tae . . . England."

Gabhran studied him for a long moment, as if he sensed Ciaran's inner turmoil over letting Isabelle go. He finally gave him a nod of farewell, stepping back.

Moments later, the manor disappeared behind them as he and Isabelle rode away. His dread had increased, and he tried not to think of their pending separation, ignoring the grief that tore at his insides.

When they arrived at Tairseach, he surveyed

the ruins of the village, an uneasy chill filling him. There was something unsettling about this place.

They dismounted, and he tied his horse to a tree before turning to Isabelle, who quietly took in the ruins.

"How does this work?" he asked, his voice unsteady.

"I'm not sure. It's like I told you before . . . there was this wind. I think—I think the wind pulled me through time somehow. I can hear it now. Can't you?"

Ciaran shook his head, looking around. An eerie stillness permeated the village; he didn't even sense the hint of a breeze.

"Ciaran," Isabelle said suddenly, stepping forward to grip his arm. "I don't want to—"

She stopped at the sound of approaching horses. Ciaran froze, turning to survey the horizon. Panic struck him at the sight of several men riding toward them. While they were too far away to identify, he suspected they were his brother's men. They must have followed them from a distance.

Ciaran cursed, grabbing Isabelle's arm.

"There's not much time. Where did ye stand—before ye were transported here?"

Shaking, Isabelle pointed to the entrance of the castle.

"But Ciaran, if those are Tavish's men—"

"I ken. 'Tis why ye need tae leave, now."

Still gripping her arm, he led her to the castle.

"Ciaran, wait. Let me help you. I don't want to go!"

Ciaran ignored her words, pulling her close to place a fervent kiss on her mouth. An array of emotions raced through him during their brief kiss —regret, fear, pain, longing.

He had to force himself to release her and step back.

"Go, Isabelle. 'Tis not safe for ye here. Live yer life. *Go.*"

Tears streamed down Isabelle's face and she shook her head. But he gently pushed her back.

"Go!" he bit out, his own tears stinging his eyes.

It happened fast. Isabelle's mouth opened, his name on her lips as she was jerked back, as if invisible arms had taken hold of her, and she . . . vanished.

Ciaran watched in horrified astonishment, reeling from her sudden disappearance. He closed his eyes, fighting against the urge to sink to his knees in grief. He regretted not telling her the words he'd wanted to say, words that came from the deepest part of him.

And so he said them now, whispering into the silence, the painful wake of her absence.

"I love ye, Isabelle."

The sound of approaching horses grew closer, and he heard the men's shouts as they spotted him.

He opened his eyes, taking a breath as he turned to face his brother's men.

CHAPTER 17

Present Day
Larkin, Scotland

The twenty-first century was a cacophony of noise.

During her initial visit to Larkin, she'd thought it was a quiet little village. But it seemed like with every passing second a loud car roared past or a plane zipped above in the sky, the distant sound of its engine reverberating throughout the streets. Even the inn itself was a hubbub of activity; the voices of various guests echoing throughout the halls, their cell phones chiming with texts and calls.

Isabelle lay in the bed of her guest room; the same guest room she'd checked into weeks ago. She closed her eyes, pulling the pillow over her head. She felt a sudden pang of longing for the relative silence of the fourteenth century; the steady clatter of horse hooves, the whisper of wind through tree branches, the patter of raindrops on the ground.

But most of all, she longed for Ciaran. Her heart clenched in her chest as she recalled the look in his eyes as he pushed her through the invisible portal—the longing and regret. The same vortex of wind that sucked her back to the past thrust her back to her own time. After a temporary suspension in darkness, she found herself in modern-day Tairseach. She could tell by the sight of her car and the difference in the trees and bushes that surrounded the village. Still, in her grief and shock she'd stumbled forward, screaming for Ciaran.

She'd almost gone back again, seeking that vortex of wind to get back to him, when a car pulled up to the side of the road, and her brother Scott stumbled out, shouting her name.

Scott had rushed to her, relief shining in his eyes, and pulled her into his arms. Later, he'd told her that the inn put him into contact with Jon after she went missing. Jon was the one who told him she may be in this area.

"Izzy."

Scott's voice pulled Isabelle from the maelstrom of her thoughts, and she turned to face him. He'd returned her to the inn, and she'd been in bed most of the time, silent and shell-shocked. She wasn't sure how much time had passed since she'd returned to the present. A day? Two?

Scott entered, his face taut with concern as he sat down next to her. Guilt swirled through her at the shadows beneath his eyes; he'd been deeply worried after she went missing. Scott had questioned her about the medieval gown she was wearing when he found her, but Isabelle hadn't told him where she'd been; she was too grief-stricken and exhausted to come up with a plausible story.

"You don't have to tell me what happened now," he said gently, as she met his eyes. "But I want to help, Iz. Please. I'm worried about you. I've never seen you like this. Is there anything I can do?"

Go back to 1390 *and save Ciaran's life. Bring him back to me. And find Fiona while you're at it,* Isabelle said silently, her chest going tight. She met her brother's eyes, the same light shade of blue as hers. How could she tell him what really happened? Scott meant well, but he'd have her sent to a psych hospital.

"I just want to be left alone," she whispered.

"Iz—"

"Please," she said. "I—I just need to rest. And then I'll to talk to you later, okay?"

Scott hesitated, but he finally got to his feet and left her room.

Once he'd left, Isabelle sat up, a renewed surge of determination flowing through her. How long was she going to languish here in her grief? If this time travel thing worked in real time, Tavish may have seized Ciaran, but there was a chance he could still be alive. She needed to get back to him.

But first she needed to make sure she did it right. For some reason, she'd ended up in Ciaran's path the last time she fell through time. She wasn't certain where she'd end up if she went back on her own now. There was someone who could get her back to the right place—the right time. Kensa.

Had she not been so grief-stricken and shell-shocked, and had her brother not shown up, she would have gone to Kensa's house and demanded that she get her back to the fourteenth century. And Isabelle would go back, but this time it wasn't just for Fiona. It was for Ciaran.

The man she loved.

She didn't realize she loved him until she returned to the present. Once it hit her that she was separated from Ciaran by centuries, her grief had incapacitated her. In the past, she knew she desired him, cared for him—but the depths of her feelings hadn't been clear until now. Feelings that now propelled her to fight for him.

She slid out of bed. She reached for a pad of stationery to scribble out a note for Scott, informing him that she needed to take a walk. And then, feeling like a prisoner making a jail break, she climbed out her window and scurried away from the inn.

Isabelle slid into her rental car, relieved that Scott had driven it back for her. She made her way to Kensa's home by memory, and when she arrived, she scrambled out of the car, hurrying to the front door and pounding on it.

No one answered. Frustrated, she moved over to the large front window, peeking in.

And her heart plummeted in her chest. The previously cluttered living room was empty as was the kitchen. The house was completely cleared out.

Tears stung at her eyes, and she stumbled back, pressing her hand to her mouth. Kensa was the one who'd made her time travel in the first place—right? Was she even able to travel back in time on her own? What if Ciaran was forever lost to her? And Fiona?

"Who lives here?"

Isabelle whirled, startled. Scott stood several yards away, leaning against his car, his arms folded across his chest with narrowed eyes.

"I followed you," he said, at her look of surprise. "Those were some nice moves, climbing out the window. You did the same thing when you were a teenager sneaking out to parties you weren't allowed to attend."

Isabelle flushed, swallowing hard as Scott approached her.

"Now's the time to talk, Izzy. I want to know where you were for all those weeks."

SCOTT PACED BACK and forth in her small guest room, his arms folded across his chest. Isabelle sat on the edge of her bed, her knees curled up to her chest, watching him with nervous anticipation.

She'd told him everything that happened from the moment Kensa came with her to Tairseach to the moment she'd returned. Now, she waited for him to tell her she was crazy, or lying, or both.

Scott finally stopped pacing to face her, dropping his hands at his sides, his expression tumultuous.

"I believe you."

Isabelle stared at him for a moment, uncertain she'd heard him right.

"What?"

"You'd never let me worry about you for weeks unless there was a good reason—and you were wearing what looked to be an authentic medieval gown when I found you. But most importantly, I saw your face when you showed up in that field. Your anguish was real. This guy—this Ciaran—I can tell he means a lot to you."

"Yes," she whispered, her throat going dry. "He did. He does. I—I don't know how to refer to him— in the present or past tense."

"Present," Scott said firmly, sitting down next to her.

Isabelle smiled, then stiffened as she realized what he'd just said.

"You said I showed up in a field. Did you not see Tairseach?"

"No. Just an open field. You did mention only people with the ability to travel can see it."

Isabelle bit her lip, considering this. Ciaran could see Tairseach. But then she remembered

Kensa's words. *In this time, only people with the ability to travel can see it.* So Tairseach was visible to everyone in the past, regardless of their time-traveling ability.

"I assume you went to Kensa's for help with returning to the past?" Scott asked.

"Yes."

She thought Scott would try to dissuade her and braced herself. Instead, he gave her a small smile.

"I know how single-minded you are, Iz," he said with a sigh. "And I know that even if I didn't help you, you'd go back anyway. I have to ask—are you sure about this? And . . . what if you can't come back?"

Isabelle considered this possibility. She wasn't certain of the answer to her brother's questions, but she was certain that she needed to get back to Ciaran. That not seeing him again was untenable.

"Then that's just a risk I'll have to take," she said.

Scott didn't look surprised. He gave her a smile filled with resolve.

"Then you know what you need to do. Tell me how I can help."

CHAPTER 18

Present Day
Inverness and Larkin, Scotland

Over the next two days, Scott became her partner in crime as she prepared to return to the fourteenth century. They were operating under the hope that she could return to the past without Kensa, though they suspected she'd used some sort of magic to help propel Isabelle through time.

Isabelle told him her theories about time travel—that Tairseach was a portal for travelers, and that time in the past occurred at the same pace as time in the present. She'd been gone for a little over a month in the present—and in the past. But that was all they had to go on, and Isabelle could only pray that when she returned, she would return to the same year.

"Are you willing to take the risk of ending up in another time?" Scott asked her grimly.

"Yes," Isabelle returned after a brief pause. "I just know that I have to try."

They drove to Inverness, where they found an antique clothing shop that sold her a fourteenth-century gown, as the gown she'd worn when she traveled back through time was now frayed by her journey.

They even went to an antique weapons store, where Scott found an old dagger authentic to the time, telling her she'd need protection.

But Scott's most important contribution was his friendship with Niall, a Scottish historian with a contact in the rare books section of the library in Inverness. He gave them access to land grant records in the Highlands from the fourteenth century, and a map of the region from the time. Isabelle thought it would be pointless, but Scott insisted it couldn't hurt to look over the records to see if there was something that could help her.

She reluctantly combed over copies of land records when they returned to the inn. She refused to go past the year 1389, not wanting to accidentally stumble across something that revealed a dark fate for Ciaran. She wouldn't accept anything other than him surviving Tavish's plot and returning to his castle as laird.

She'd been reviewing the records for nearly two hours—and was on the verge of giving up—when a familiar name caught her eye. She froze, her finger running over the scrawled words. It detailed the ceding of lands by a T of Clan Aitharne to a Walrick of the same clan.

She scrambled to her feet, leaving her room to knock on her brother's door.

"I think the T stands for Tavish, Ciaran's brother," she said, showing Scott the record when he let her in. "He's ceding land to someone. I may not know much about clans and how things worked back then, but—"

"Ceding land is something only lairds or men with property of their own could do," Scott concluded.

"Exactly. Ciaran was laird in 1389, not Tavish. If Tavish was granting land to people when he shouldn't have—an entire year before he set Ciaran up for murder—this may be proof. It shows that Tavish was paying someone off . . . possibly to lie for him," Isabelle said, her heart hammering. "Scott . . . what if this is what Ciaran needs to clear his name?"

"Then you've found your smoking gun," Scott confirmed.

THEY DETERMINED that Isabelle would attempt to return to the past the next day. Scott suggested they grab dinner at a small restaurant in town, which served "authentic Highland fare" according to the smiling woman who owned it.

They ate in silence over their meal of Scotch broth and shortbread, until Scott set down his fork.

"So. You go back, you successfully rescue Ciaran and find Fiona. Then what? Do you come back?"

Isabelle stilled. She had already experienced life in the fourteenth century and acclimated to it quite well. And the time period could use her teaching skills, given how common illiteracy was. But most importantly, the thought of finding Ciaran—only to leave him again—was incomprehensible.

Scott saw the answer in her eyes and gave her a small nod.

"I already knew your answer. I just had to make sure. If you do stay, I can take care of things for you in Chicago—your apartment and job. You won't have to worry about that. I can tell you love him, Iz," he said, giving her a sad smile. "I'd have loved a chance to meet the guy who's stolen my little sister's heart."

"I don't know if he feels the same way," Isabelle replied, a stab of insecurity piercing her. "He'll probably be angry with me for returning and insist that I come back to my own time. But I'd never be able to live with myself if I didn't try."

"I know," Scott said, reaching across the table to squeeze her hand.

"Scottie," she said, a rush of warmth filling her heart as she used her childhood nickname for her brother. Scott had always been there for her; she'd lucked out by having him as a brother. "Thank you for believing me. And for helping me."

"Hey," Scott said, leaning forward in his chair. "I made you a promise after Mom and Dad died, remember? I promised I'd protect you and do everything I could to make sure you were happy. I may not be able to protect you in the past, but if this man makes you happy, I can help you get back to him."

Though she was reassured by Scott's words, that night she couldn't sleep. What if she couldn't travel through time without Kensa? What if she ended up in a different place? A different time? And an even darker thought plagued her. What if it was already too late to save Ciaran, and he'd already been executed?

A strangled sob erupted from her at the thought, and she pressed her hand to her mouth. She wouldn't let herself entertain it.

She finally managed to get a small amount of sleep, crawling out of bed just after dawn to dress in her medieval gown, stowing the dagger securely beneath her sleeve. Scott's eyes widened when he came to her room to collect her.

"Well, you certainly look the part, Iz," he said with a grin.

They drove to Tairseach in silence, Isabelle having to point out where to stop once she spotted its ruins.

When they climbed out of the car, Scott gave her the longest embrace he'd ever given her—even longer than the one he'd given her after they lost their parents.

"Be safe, Izzy," he whispered, when he released her. "I love you."

"I love you too," she said, blinking back tears. "If I do stay in the past, I'll find a way to visit you. I promise."

"Good. But even if you don't . . . I just want your happiness. And it sounds like your Highlander makes you happy. Now go. Go rescue the man you love."

It was an echo of the words Ciaran had spoken, right before he pushed her back through time. *Live yer life. Go.* But what she'd realized in that moment was that her life was with Ciaran.

Isabelle smiled, giving her brother one last look before she turned to enter the village. She could feel Scott's eyes on her as she made her way to the same spot she'd come to with Kensa.

She took a deep breath as the wind picked up, and unlike the other two times she'd traveled, when she'd felt uncertainty and fear—this time there was only determination. Determination and love.

Ciaran, she thought, her heart swelling as she saw the man she loved in her mind's eye.

She closed her eyes, allowing the wind to suck her back through the chasm of time.

1390
Aitharne Castle

Ciaran wondered if Isabelle and the time he'd spent with her at Gabhran's manor had all been a dream.

He was back in the same cell he'd languished in weeks before, despair seeping into his bones. He kept seeing Isabelle vanish right before his eyes.

After she'd disappeared, Tavish's men had hauled him back to Aitharne Castle. Tavish told Ciaran he'd found him by having his men watch Gabhran's manor in case he returned there.

"Yet the whole time, ye were hiding out in his manor like a coward. Now tell me," Tavish had hissed, as soon as a guard threw Ciaran into the cell. "Where is that Sassenach with the strange tongue who lied tae me? She needs tae be punished for her deception."

But Ciaran had remained silent, relieved that Isabelle was safe in her own time, free from Tavish's wrath. He thought Tavish would resort to torture to get answers from him, but to Ciaran's relief he'd stopped questioning him about Isabelle after his first day of captivity. Ciaran assumed—hoped—that Tavish was content with his capture. Ciaran was the one he wanted dead.

Ciaran closed his eyes, taking a shuddering breath. He didn't know how long he'd been in this cell. He'd passed the time by thinking of Isabelle. The musical sound of her laughter, the way her blue eyes lit up when she discussed something she was passionate about, the softness of her bare skin against his as he made love to her.

A wave of grief swept over him. His former goal to avenge Eoin and clear his name had vanished along with Isabelle. Isabelle, who had so briefly shone a light onto the darkness of his life, was no longer with him. She was gone, like his brother, and darkness was the only thing that fed his dispirited soul.

Now he longed for it to all to be over. He hoped to carry his memories of Isabelle with him into death. Love had been a foreign concept to him; he'd not come close to loving any of the lasses he'd bedded before. But he knew that love described the depths of his feelings for Isabelle. She was the only lass he had ever or would ever love, and she was now lost to him across the expanse of time.

Ciaran drifted off to sleep, coming to off and

on, barely touching the gruel the guard shoved into his cell. He didn't recognize this guard, a stocky man with severe gray eyes who spoke in grunts and barks. He didn't know what had become of Angus; he could only pray that Tavish hadn't punished him with death for releasing him. Nor was there any sign of Lachaid, whom Ciaran was certain would have visited him by now. Ciaran prayed that he too was safe.

The guard shook him awake from one of his brief sleeps, one filled with images of his Isabelle. The guard roughly lifted him to his feet, and he realized with a dark relief that this was it, he was finally being marched to his death.

His legs were weak from his long spell of sitting; he struggled to walk with the guard, who led him out of the dungeons. He noticed that the corridors of the castle seemed quiet; the castle always grew quiet when there was an execution. He never thought it would one day be a witness to his own.

The guard kept a firm grip on his arm as he led him out to the courtyard. A small crowd was gathered; Ciaran recognized some familiar faces, ranging from castle workers to local villagers.

Tavish stood on the scaffold he'd had built for this occasion, next to the hangman and a noose. Ciaran searched his brother's eyes for any regret or guilt, but he only saw burning hatred as the guard led him up the scaffold's steps.

Ciaran felt nothing but a numb resolve as the

hangman stepped forward, placing the noose around his neck. Tavish stepped forward to address the crowd.

"My brother, your former laird and former chieftain of Clan Aitharne, stands guilty of the murder of my dear brother, Eoin," Tavish announced. "After his cowardly escape, I have returned him to the castle for his punishment—death by hanging."

The crowd reacted with silence, not the usual jeers or cries that accompanied hangings. Ciaran had been a kind laird to the villagers and castle workers; he could see disbelief and grief in many of their eyes.

Tavish scowled, looking displeased by the lack of acclamation from his announcement.

"Today ye are not the favored one, beloved by all," Tavish hissed in a low voice, turning to face Ciaran. "Today ye go tae yer death like a traitor and criminal. The clan and castle will be mine; I will do everything I can tae stamp out your memory."

If Ciaran could feel anything, he would have recoiled from the spite in Tavish's eyes, though a part of him wanted to laugh.

How had he not seen this before? Tavish's hatred stemmed from jealousy. Jealousy that Ciaran was chief and laird, that he was a well-liked leader. It was this jealousy that led him to kill Eoin, leaving all the inherited power to him.

But Ciaran chose not to react to his brother's words; he wouldn't give him the pleasure of a response. He stared straight ahead, filling his mind with thoughts of Isabelle as the hangman tightened the noose around his neck, and Tavish stepped down from the scaffold.

Isabelle's warm hand in his as they walked through the gardens of Gabhran's estate. Isabelle's laughter as he told her of his and Gabhran's youthful exploits. Isabelle telling him about the works of a poet not yet born named William Shakespeare, her voice infused with passion as she recited some of his poetry: "*When Love speaks, the voice of all the gods makes heaven drowsy with the harmony.*"

I love ye, Isabelle, he thought, closing his eyes as the hangman stepped back. Bracing himself for the end.

The sound of multiple horse hooves and startled shouts forced his eyes open.

Two dozen men rode into the courtyard, scattering the gathered crowd. Ciaran watched in dazed disbelief, recognizing two of the riders—Gabhran and Lachaid—as they dismounted from their horses, withdrawing their swords to fight off Tavish's men.

Amid the chaos, several riders rode toward him, a cloak shielding one of their faces. As the rider drew closer, Ciaran's heart stopped.

The rider wasn't a man. It was Isabelle.

The other men who rode with her leapt from their horses, charging at Tavish and the hangman. Tavish, who had gone still and white with shock, stumbled back as the men charged toward him, calling fearfully for his guards.

The hangman turned to flee while one of Ciaran's rescuers cut him free from the noose.

Isabelle remained on her horse, extending her hand.

"Ciaran!" she shouted. "Come with me! Get on my horse!"

This isnae real, Ciaran thought in a daze. *I've already died, and this is just—*

"Ciaran!" Isabelle shouted again. "We have to leave!"

The man who'd freed him from his noose gave him a gentle shove, and Ciaran stepped off of the scaffold, climbing onto the back of Isabelle's horse. She kicked the sides of her horse, and they tore out of the courtyard as Tavish's men continued to fight off Ciaran's rescuers.

Shock tore through him as they rode, and he tightened his arms around Isabelle's waist—both to keep himself steady and to reassure himself that she was real. He took in the long, silky, dark strands of her hair, leaning forward to inhale her familiar honeyed scent. Tears stung his eyes; it was her. His Isabelle.

He tightened his grip on her waist as they continued to ride. Ciaran fought against his weakness and fatigue as they rode, not wanting to fall asleep only to wake back up in that cell, to find that this had all been a glorious dream.

Isabelle stopped when they reached a crumbling old manor deep in the Highlands, one he didn't recognize. She dismounted and gently helped him down.

He swayed on his feet, reaching out to touch her face. She caught his hands in hers and met his eyes, tears glistening in her own.

"Isabelle," he breathed. "My Isabelle."

He wanted to kiss her, to pull her into his arms and never let her go, but he could no longer fight off his fatigue, and succumbed to the blackness that claimed him.

$\mathcal{C}$iaran came to in a large chamber. He lay in the center of a bed, with Isabelle sitting at his side. She stroked his hair, placing a cup of water to his lips.

"Drink," she murmured. "You're dehydrated."

He drank, relishing in the feel of the liquid flowing down his throat, his eyes locked on Isabelle's the entire time, his heart leaping with joy. He'd feared he'd awake back in his cell, or that he was already dead.

But Isabelle was at his side, dressed in a lovely gown of deep lavender, her raven hair hanging loose around her shoulders, her blue eyes filled with concern as she watched him drink.

"You're here," he whispered, when he'd drunk his fill, and she set down the cup on the side table. "How?"

"I couldn't leave you here to die for a crime you

didn't commit. And I still haven't found Fiona," Isabelle said. "I had to come back."

He shook his head, overwhelmed with disbelief at her bravery, at her daring that bordered on the foolish.

"How'd ye find me?"

"I was able to travel back again—on my own. I arrived in Tairseach. I got a map of this area in my time. I got a horse at a nearby village and went right back to Gabhran and Donella's manor—they were still there. I told them I turned back at the border and couldn't bear to leave you behind. They sent for your friend Lachaid when I told them about Tavish capturing you; Lachaid came with about twenty men loyal to you from your clan and Gabhran's. We all planned the rescue. I didn't want to wait until the day you were scheduled to hang, but Lachaid told me it was easiest to rescue you when you were out in the open. I—I was afraid we'd be too late," she whispered, reaching out to touch the side of his face. She expelled a shaky breath, gesturing around at the chamber. "We're at the manor of Lachaid's late uncle. He said Tavish doesn't know about this place—hardly anyone does."

Ciaran studied her with admiration. But as joyful as he was to see her, unease spiraled through him.

"I'm glad tae see ye again. But 'tis dangerous for ye here. 'Tis why I insisted ye return tae yer time. Tavish is determined tae see me hang—and determined tae find ye. Now that ye've helped me escape, he—"

"I've traveled back six hundred years through time," Isabelle interrupted with a scowl. "I'm not letting fear of your spoiled little brother stop me from helping you—and from finding my best friend."

Ciaran knew he should insist that she go back to her time, but she was looking at him with a fiery determination, as if daring him to challenge her.

He smiled, reaching for her hand and lifting it to his lips for a kiss. He didn't want her to go . . . for purely selfish reasons. He wanted her at his side and in his bed—not just for now, but for always, though he knew that was impossible. She didn't belong in this time, and she would one day return to her own.

"I missed ye, lass," he murmured, pushing the painful thought away. "I dreamed of ye the entire time I was in my cell."

Isabelle's expression softened.

"I missed you too," she whispered. "I was afraid I'd never see you again."

He pulled her close, claiming her mouth with his own. Warmth and desire coiled around him as he tasted her, relishing in the feel of her in his arms once more. His cock swelled as he pulled her closer, unable to quell the need that filled him at her proximity.

But Isabelle shifted, releasing herself from his kiss with a guilty flush.

"Ciaran, you're still weak," she whispered. "And you've not eaten. We should wait until—"

He silenced her with a kiss, pulling her down next to him. Isabelle whimpered in protest at first, but wrapped her arms around his neck, probing his mouth with the same eagerness with which his mouth probed hers.

"Right now, I only hunger for ye, my beauty," he whispered, releasing her mouth from his. He lowered the bodice of her gown, swallowing at the sight of her firm breasts. "I dreamed about every part of yer lovely body while I was imprisoned. Yer ripe breasts . . ."

He leaned down, seizing her nipple with his mouth and suckling. Isabelle moaned as he nursed on one breast, and then the other.

"The plane of yer stomach," he continued, stripping her of her gown before kissing down the expanse of her abdomen.

Isabelle bit her lip, stifling a moan as he peppered his kisses lower . . . lower still. She cried out as his mouth found her center, and he feasted on her.

"The taste of honey between yer thighs," he growled, as he licked and probed her center, until she shuddered her release.

"Ciaran . . ." she whimpered, when she came back to earth.

"I'm not finished, lass," he replied, nipping at the base of her throat as he lifted himself from her center, removing his kilt as he positioned himself above her. "I dreamed of the feel of ye . . . when I buried myself inside ye."

Isabelle gasped as he sank himself inside her, her eyes widening as he began to move. He increased the force of his thrusts as pleasure built up within him, his eyes roaming from Isabelle's flushed face to her bouncing breasts, burying his face in her neck as their mutual pleasure built to a climax, and he shouted her name as he came, spilling himself inside her.

"But most of all, my beauty," he whispered, when he had again caught his breath, leaning down to seize her lips with his own. "I missed yer smile. Yer laughter. Ye."

Isabelle's expression filled with warmth.

"I felt like Orpheus when I returned," she murmured. "Returning to the underworld to save you."

He smiled, holding her close as he reached out to tuck a stray strand of hair behind her ear. It wasn't a confession of love, but hearing that Isabelle cared for him was enough to make his heart swell.

"Are the Highlands the underworld, lass?" he teased. "Are they that bad compared tae yer time?"

"You know what I mean," Isabelle said, reaching out to give him a playful swat.

"I was happy tae have ye rescue me," he said, in all seriousness. "I was bereft of hope till I saw ye again. My Isabelle."

Isabelle rested her head on his shoulder, and he pulled her even closer, wanting nothing more than to bind her to him. She may not belong in this time, but that didn't mean he couldn't enjoy the time he had with her, and he intended to savor every moment.

Just after first light the next morning, Ciaran stood by the window, gazing out at the grounds of the manor. It was hard to believe that just the day before, he'd been prepared for death. Had longed for it.

He turned to Isabelle, who lay sleeping in bed. Her dark hair had fallen over her face in the throes of sleep, and the rise and fall of her chest was steady with her breaths. Her return had rejuvenated him; his determination reawakened. Shame filled him at his dark and suicidal thoughts of the day before. Why had he allowed himself to face defeat? Never again. He would confront Tavish and take back his birthright.

Isabelle stirred, her lovely eyes fluttering open. He crossed the chamber to sit at her side, pulling her into the circle of his arms. He would have to go downstairs to talk to Lachaid and Gabhran about what he planned to do, and to thank them for his rescue. But for now, he wanted to enjoy these few moments alone with his Isabelle.

"Before you talk to the others, there's something you should know," Isabelle murmured, looking up at him. "In my time, I found something of note in an archive. It was a record of Tavish granting land to a noble named Walrick last year."

Ciaran stiffened, releasing her. Walrick had been one of the men to make false statements against him in Eoin's murder.

"Do you know him?" Isabelle asked, holding his gaze.

"Aye," he said grimly. "I do. He provided false testimony that helped convict me of my brother's murder."

"Then this is proof," Isabelle said, her eyes widening. "Proof that you can use."

"I'd need some record of the deed which may prove difficult. But aye," he said, getting to his feet. "If I can get it—and get it to the other nobles of my clan—it would help me."

Moments later, he and Isabelle went downstairs to greet the men who'd rescued him. Some he recognized from his clan; low-born men who tilled the fields of Aitharne lands; they'd remained loyal to him as he'd always been fair with the rents he collected. Others were Gabhran's men; they'd come to his aid on Gabhran's word alone.

He thanked them all before pulling Gabhran and Lachaid aside to privately express his gratitude. Relief filled Ciaran when Gabhran told him he'd sent Donella and their daughter to relatives who lived in Edinburgh; they'd be safe there while he was away.

After he told them what he'd learned about Walrick, they both went pale.

"That scheming bastard," Gabhran hissed. "Smiling tae yer face, pretending tae be yer friend, all the while plotting against ye."

"It fills me with rage what he did, but we can use this," Ciaran said. "I cannae get tae the other nobles my brother paid off in the castle. But I can get tae Walrick. I'll offer him more lands when I regain my title if he tells the nobles of my clan what Tavish did."

"Admitting to his own guilt?" Isabelle interjected with a frown. "Why would he do that?"

"The lass is right," Gabhran said. "He's proven he cannae be trusted. How do ye ken he'll not just turn ye in?"

"Because I can offer him more lands than my brother can, and that's all he cares about. 'Tis the best chance I have of clearing my name," Ciaran said.

"Even if this does work—how do we get tae him?" Lachaid asked.

"I used tae hunt with him. He goes hunting at midday with only his two sons. We can surround him when he's in a remote area and bring him here. Once here, I'll convince him tae agree."

A long silence fell. Isabelle, Gabhran, and Lachaid all looked uncertain. He knew his plan was risky, but he didn't have an array of choices.

"I suppose 'tis the best way of clearing yer name," Lachaid finally said, shaking his head. "When do ye want tae ride?"

"Tomorrow. We can follow him from his manor right when he leaves," Ciaran said.

Gabhran and Lachaid left to inform the other men of their plan. Isabelle moved close to his side, taking his hand in hers, her face tight with worry.

"What's wrong, lass?"

"I'm worried that your plan will backfire."

"Backfire?" he asked, his brows knitting together in a confused frown at the strange term.

"Not go according to plan," Isabelle amended. "I just wish there was some way of knowing he won't turn you in or betray you."

"'Tis a risk I must take. I want Eoin avenged and my life back," he said, placing his hand on the side of her face.

Then I'll have a life tae offer ye, he added silently. *Then perhaps I can convince ye tae stay in a time ye doonae belong, even if 'tis selfish tae ask, with the man who will always love ye.*

CHAPTER 21

*I*sabelle paced restlessly in her guest chamber. Ciaran and most of the men had left after first light to confront Walrick. She'd wanted to come along, but Ciaran had summarily refused. Unlike the castle rescue, of which she'd been a vital part, he and the others insisted she would only get in the way.

"And I'd just want tae protect ye, lass, when I need tae focus," Ciaran had insisted.

So he'd left her behind with several burly Highlanders as her guards. Ciaran had given them strict instructions to return her to Tairseach should anything go awry, ignoring her protests.

She expelled a sigh, looking around her large, dank guest chamber. She hated feeling useless. Even her search for Fiona had come to a standstill; there was nothing she could do to resume that search until she had access to another messenger. Ciaran had assured her that once he had his title returned, he'd do everything in his power to help her locate Fiona.

Isabelle moved to the window, looking out for the millionth time. She didn't know exactly how long it had been since they'd all left, but midday had come and gone, and she'd barely eaten the two small meals of bread and stew a guard brought to her chamber. She had no appetite; she wouldn't be able to eat a single bite until she knew Ciaran was safe.

Isabelle stilled when she heard the rumble of horses approaching the manor. She whirled, hurrying out of the chamber to make her way downstairs. She ignored the cautioning shouts of one of the guards as she threw open the front door.

Her chest filled with relief at the sight of Ciaran riding alongside Gabhran, Lachaid and the others. A scowling red-haired man and two other men with similar features rode with them; she assumed this was Walrick and his sons.

She stepped forward as the men dismounted. Gabhran and his men kept hold of Walrick and his two sons, marching with them into the manor.

"What happened?" Isabelle asked, once she reached Ciaran.

"They came with not much of a fight, but it will be difficult tae get Walrick tae work with us," Ciaran said.

"And if he does?"

"We're arranging tae meet with Ramsey, a noble from my clan who still holds me in high regard. If

Walrick tells him what Tavish has done, Ramsey will inform the other nobles."

"Then your name will be cleared?"

"If all goes well," Ciaran said, but he didn't look so certain.

He's right to be cautious, Isabelle thought, with a sliver of unease. So many things could still go wrong. Walrick could turn on him. This other noble from his clan could turn on him. Or Tavish's men could storm the manor at any moment and capture them all.

"Doonae worry yerself with all this, lass," Ciaran said, studying her strained features. "'Tis not yer concern. If anything should happen, ye return tae where 'tis safe."

His eyes held hers, and Isabelle understood his meaning. She bit her lip, frustration roiling through her gut. She thought she'd been clear when she told him she wasn't leaving until she helped clear his name and located Fiona. But it seemed like her words had fallen on deaf ears.

Before she could raise any objection to his words, he raised her hand to his lips in a quick kiss before leaving to deal with Walrick.

She trailed after him, only to nearly collide with Lachaid. She apologized and started to move past him, but his words stopped her.

"May I ask ye something, lass?"

"Of course," Isabelle said, though she stiffened with wary caution. She'd told Lachaid the same backstory she'd told everyone else, but she feared he'd ask her for more details.

"Why are ye doing so much tae help Ciaran?"

Isabelle flushed, swallowing hard. Now she wished he'd asked her for details about where she was from. Anything besides having to discuss her love for Ciaran.

"Ye could have been safe in England," Lachaid continued, his dark eyes probing hers. "Instead, ye risked yer life tae come back and rescue him."

"I owe him my life for saving me from those bandits," Isabelle said stiffly.

Lachaid gave her a look that was half skepticism, half disbelief.

"Ciaran hasnae had a lass in his life before ye," Lachaid said, after a long pause. "He's had mistresses, aye, and before this mess with Tavish, the nobles were pressuring him tae marry. And he would have done so for the sake of his clan."

Isabelle's heart clenched; she had to suppress the jealousy that coursed through her at his words. Why had she not considered this before? Ciaran was a fourteenth-century Highland laird. Wouldn't he be required to marry the daughter of a fellow Scottish noble? A time-traveling high school English teacher hardly fit the bill of a suitable bride.

"But," Lachaid continued, "he wouldnae have been happy. I've watched him around ye. I've never seen such light in his eyes. He's suffered since Eoin's death . . . 'tis as if ye've brought him back tae life. I ken Ciaran, and he's a man of honor. He may try tae push ye away because of this business with his brother. I say . . . doonae let him."

Lachaid gave her a kind smile before leaving her alone to ponder his words. Did he somehow sense her true feelings for Ciaran? And if he had, could that mean Ciaran suspected her feelings as well?

THAT EVENING, she found Ciaran in her guest chamber, looking out the window.

"I doonae think Walrick will cooperate," Ciaran said, turning to face her as she entered.

"Isabelle . . ." He hesitated, his eyes shadowing. "I may continue tae be an outlaw for some time. How long are ye willing tae stay in this time tae help me?"

Lachaid was right, Isabelle thought, impressed by his foresight that Ciaran would try to push her away. But then again, it was what she'd expected. Hadn't Ciaran already forced her to return to her own time?

"As long as it takes," she said firmly. She couldn't fathom going back to the future and leaving Ciaran to an uncertain fate. During the brief time she'd been back in the present she'd felt adrift, like a sailor far away from any shore. She suspected that was how she'd always feel in a time without Ciaran.

Ciaran stiffened for a moment before his expression softened.

"My Isabelle," he murmured, his eyes filling with admiration. "What did I do tae deserve such a lass? Do ye ken . . . I've had fantasies of how I would've courted ye had we met under different circumstances."

"Really?" she asked, delight rippling through her. He would have courted her, even though she wasn't the daughter of a noble? "How would you have courted me?"

"First," he said, pulling her into his arms as he turned back to the window, pressing her back against the hard line of his chest, "I would've had ye come tae the castle for a feast. I would've had the cook make ye my favorite meal—roasted pork with a sweet wine. And then I would've taken ye on a walk around the castle grounds . . . shown ye the garden my mother planted. I would've then called on ye every day, taken ye on rides in the forest that lay just beyond the castle and around the surrounding moors. I would've taken ye on more long walks, not just around the castle, but around the nearby loch and the forests, and have ye tell me details of all yer favorite tales."

"And then?" Isabelle pressed, closing her eyes as she imagined this glorious alternate timeline.

Ciaran turned her around to face him. She opened her eyes, and heat spiraled around her at the intense look in his hazel eyes.

"Then I would've asked for yer hand," he whispered.

Isabelle wasn't prepared for the surge of joy that filled her at his words. She knew she would have said yes to such a proposal in a heartbeat and given up her life in the present to stay with Ciaran.

"And only then," he whispered, pulling her even closer, his eyes dropping to her mouth, "would I have taken ye tae my bed and worshipped yer lovely body as it is meant tae be worshipped."

She gasped as he swung her up into his arms.

"None of those things can happen while I'm an outlaw," he murmured. "Except for the worship. And that I intend tae do as much as possible."

Desire seeped into every part of her, and she pressed her mouth to his as he carried her to the bed, where he thoroughly fulfilled his promise.

CHAPTER 22

*E*arly the next morning, Ciaran stood in the small chamber where they were holding Walrick, glaring at the man he'd once considered a friend. Walrick, who sat tied up in a chair, returned his glare, his gray eyes filled with hatred.

Ciaran expelled a breath, frustration filling him. If only he'd seen Walrick's greed, his self-serving nature, when they were friends. He'd shared many hunting trips and feasts with him, and he'd considered Walrick a jovial and kindhearted man. But he'd helped Tavish get away with Eoin's murder—all for the sake of extra land.

He clenched his fists at his sides to quell his anger. He allowed his thoughts to drift to the one person who calmed him: Isabelle. After making love the night before, they'd lain entwined in each other's arms, speaking of their hopes for the future he'd painted. He'd feared his confession of wanting to wed her would have frightened her, but he only saw delight in her eyes at his words.

Isabelle was the only light that had emerged from the darkness of his brother's betrayal. There was a time he would have never considered marrying a lass not allied with his clan. The marriages of lairds were often arranged among high-ranking families; it was important to keep lands and properties consolidated. Even his parents' marriage had been arranged by their families; they'd eventually come to love each other on their own. Ciaran always assumed he'd have an arranged marriage, and he never would have expected to fall in love with his bride. Not the way he'd fallen in love with his Isabelle.

"Treacherous bastard."

Walrick's words pulled Ciaran back to the present, and his anger returned. He'd tried to reason with Walrick. While it had been relatively easy to surround and capture Walrick while he was out on his hunt, Walrick nor his two sons had been cooperative, and he doubted Walrick would tell the visiting noble Ramsey of Tavish's treachery. But Ciaran had no other option; he had to convince Walrick to work with him.

"Ye speak of yerself when ye use the word treacherous," Ciaran growled. He knew that Walrick just wanted to cause him ire, but his words still had their intended effect. "Was it easy for ye tae betray me for lands? To conspire in a murder?"

"I do what I must for my family—for my sons,"

Walrick returned. "I couldnae turn down what Tavish offered."

Ciaran tensed, aching to reach for his sword and sink his blade into Walrick's chest. This man's actions had allowed Eoin's death to go unpunished. Ciaran had to force his rage to subside before continuing.

"Ramsey, a noble from our clan who ye ken, is coming here. Ye need tae tell him about yer dealings with Tavish. All ye have tae do is tell him the truth, and then ye'll go free."

"Or ye'll do what?" Walrick hissed, glowering at him. "We both ken ye're no murderer, Ciaran. Yer honor has always been yer downfall."

Ciaran gritted his teeth, but Walrick was right. Gabhran and the others had wanted to threaten Walrick with the death of his sons to get him to talk, but Ciaran refused. Despite what Tavish had done, Ciaran couldn't bring himself to commit murder, even to clear his own name.

But Walrick didn't need to know that.

"Ye doonae ken what I'm capable of," Ciaran snapped, taking a threatening step forward. "Just tell Ramsey the truth, and ye'll go free."

Ciaran turned to leave, but Walrick's next words stopped him cold.

"'Tis a fine lassie ye have stowed away here," Walrick purred. "I could've sworn I heard her moans last night. Are her services just for ye, or do ye share her with yer men?"

Ciaran couldn't control the hot fury that struck

him at Walrick's words. He withdrew his sword and crossed the chamber in three long strides, grabbing Walrick by the collar and raising his blade.

"Ciaran!"

A restraining hand was placed on his arm, pulling him back. Ciaran turned, his teeth clenched and his breathing ragged. Gabhran stood directly behind him.

"What are ye doing?" Gabhran snapped. "We need him alive."

"I asked about the services of his whore," Walrick said recklessly, and Ciaran charged at him again. But Gabhran kept his hand firmly around Ciaran's arms, dragging him out of the chamber.

"He's trying tae goad ye, and ye're letting him," Gabhran hissed, when they were out in the hallway.

Ciaran closed his eyes, taking several deep breaths as his anger subsided. He knew Walrick's intention, but it didn't change the state of his fury.

"I'm sorry," he muttered.

"Doonae go near him until Ramsey arrives," Gabhran said with a scowl. His expression softened as he continued, "We're trying tae clear yer name. The men here are risking their lives tae help ye. Doonae let his goading make ye lose sight of that."

Guilt filled him at Gabhran's words, and he gave him a sharp nod.

Still, he had to walk around the grounds that surrounded the manor to calm himself, cursing himself for his temper. He usually fared well when calming himself, but when it came to threats against his Isabelle . . . calm was difficult to maintain.

Isabelle found him while he walked, taking his hand and walking with him in companionable silence. If she wondered about his state of agitation, she said nothing about it, allowing him to further calm down before he spoke.

"I'm on edge about Ramsey's visit," Ciaran finally said. She didn't need to know about Walrick's foul words. "I ken I doonae have much choice, but if Walrick continues tae not cooperate—"

"Don't worry about that now," Isabelle urged. "There's nothing you can do until he arrives."

She pointedly changed the subject, asking him about his connection to the men who were here. He knew she was trying to distract him from his troubles, and it worked as he told her about his long-term friendship with Lachaid, and how he knew some of the men who'd come to his aid.

By the time they'd finished their walk and returned to the manor, he'd fully calmed down and was ready for Ramsey's visit.

"Ye need tae go tae yer chamber during Ramsey's visit," he told Isabelle. "Please, for yer safety. I doonae want ye near in case things go awry."

Isabelle looked torn, but she gave him a jerky nod. He walked her to her chamber, making certain she went inside and two men stood outside her door.

Ramsey arrived moments later, his horse riding up to the manor. Ciaran held himself stiffly as Ramsey dismounted and approached.

Ramsey ducked his head in a respectful bow at the sight of him.

"My laird," Ramsey said. "'Tis good tae see ye."

Surprise filled him; he'd expected subtle hostility and distrust from his former noble.

"I believe in yer innocence, and I'm not the only one," Ramsey said, at Ciaran's look of surprise. "All we need is proof."

"And I hope tae give it tae ye," Ciaran said. "Come."

He led Ramsey into the drawing room where two of their men held Walrick between them in a firm grip.

"I understand ye have something ye want tae tell me about Tavish," Ramsey said.

The silence in the room stretched as Walrick held Ramsey's gaze, before his cold eyes slid to Ciaran.

"This treacherous bastard is holding me and my sons against my will," Walrick bit out. "They want me tae tell ye something that isnae true. He murdered his brother and wants tae—"

"Ye bastard!" Ciaran snarled, his calm shattered as he charged toward Walrick. This time it took both Gabhran and Lachaid to hold him back.

"Look at that temper!" Walrick shouted. "Is

that why ye killed Eoin? Did he say or do something tae anger ye? Or maybe ye just wanted tae hold on tae power?"

"Get him out of here!" Gabhran hissed, and the men hauled the sneering Walrick from the room.

Ciaran closed his eyes as Lachaid and Gabhran released him, defeat settling over him like a great weight. How foolish he'd been to assume Walrick would help him, even for lands. The bastard had shown him nothing but hostility ever since they'd captured him. It had been a desperate and risky plan; he should have better anticipated this outcome.

"I was hoping he would tell me something I could tell the other nobles," Ramsey said, giving Ciaran a sorrowful look. "Ye should ken—Tavish is searching high and low for ye. He intends tae hang not just ye, but all who have helped ye as well."

Ciaran's chest tightened. He knew this, but hearing the words out loud still filled him with fear. He thought of Gabhran, of Lachaid, of the brave men who'd helped him.

But most of all, he thought of his love. His Isabelle. He would do anything to keep her safe— even if it meant giving up his life. Even if it meant Eoin's death would go unavenged.

"I understand. I thank ye, Ramsey," Ciaran said quietly.

"If there's anything more I can do tae help, just send me a message," Ramsey said, before taking his leave. "I ken it doesnae seem like it, but ye still have friends at the castle."

Everyone gathered in the drawing room after Ramsey left; Isabelle joined them as well. As soon as she met his eyes, Isabelle crossed the room to him.

"Gabhran just told me what happened," she whispered. "I'm so sorry, Ciaran."

"We'll not give up," Lachaid said, from across the room. "There are others who can help. It may take time, but—"

"No," Ciaran interrupted.

Everyone fell silent, looking at him with concern. At his side, Isabelle stiffened.

He took a breath and swallowed. He wouldn't let Isabelle or his friends come to harm because of him. Walrick had been his last hope. It was time to end this.

"I've a different plan, one many of ye willnae like."

Isabelle took a step back, already looking as if she were on the verge of protest.

Ciaran forced his gaze away from her, making himself say the difficult words.

"I'm going tae get my brother tae confess tae his crimes, but it will take a sacrifice. Me."

CHAPTER 23

Icy dread coursed through Isabelle's veins as Ciaran told them his plan.

"I'll meet Tavish under the guise of being alone," he said. "I'll goad him till he reveals what he's done. We'll arrange tae have the other clan nobles listening in, out of sight. I can then have him arrested."

Isabelle looked at him in disbelief, and the other men in the room fell silent. They looked just as shocked as she felt. After several long moments, the men all burst into a chorus of protests.

"Yer brother will never confess tae murdering Eoin!" Lachaid cried.

"And how do ye even propose we get inside the castle without being seen?" Gabhran demanded.

"Tavish has men everywhere—how are we tae get the other nobles to listen in?" another man by the name of Kelan demanded.

But Isabelle couldn't find words of her own,

she was too flabbergasted. His plan was reckless and dangerous. Was he trying to get himself killed?

Ciaran settled his hazel eyes on her, as if waiting for her to speak. When she remained quiet, he held up his hands for silence.

"I'll discuss this with ye all later," he said, addressing the men but looking at Isabelle. "I need a moment alone with Isabelle."

The men obliged with grumbles of protest. Once she and Ciaran were alone, Isabelle finally found her voice.

"Are you mad, Ciaran?" she demanded. "Do you know what your brother will do as soon as you're in his sights? You'll be on the scaffold before you can even speak!"

"Isabelle—"

"Ciaran . . . I love you."

A look of astonishment flashed across Ciaran's face. She'd not wanted to confess her feelings for him like this, in a time of desperation. But given that he was on the verge of risking his life with a foolish plan, she had nothing to lose.

"Isabelle . . ." he repeated, his eyes filling with emotion as he stepped toward her.

"Let me finish. You don't know what it did to me, to see you on that scaffold with a noose tied around your neck," Isabelle continued, her voice wavering at the memory. "It—it nearly broke me, Ciaran. Don't you understand? I came back through time not just to rescue you and find Fiona

—but to *be* with you. I love you, and I can't watch you risk your life."

Tears blurred her vision as fear seized her; fear at the thought of losing Ciaran. Ciaran reached out to pull her within the circle of his arms.

"Doonae weep, lass. I cannae bear tae see ye in pain."

"Then tell me you're not going to do this."

She looked at him with pleading eyes, but Ciaran's expression remained firm—and apologetic. Isabelle closed her eyes, her heart splintering in her chest. He wasn't going to back down.

"I love ye, Isabelle."

Isabelle's eyes flew open. Ciaran was looking at her with utter sincerity—with love. It was the words she'd hoped he'd say to her. Even when he mentioned wanting to wed her, he'd not spoken of love. Under different circumstances, an overwhelming joy would have filled her at his words. Instead, her anguish only increased.

Why couldn't they have met in the future, when everything was far safer? Why couldn't they exist in a time and place where they could just . . . be?

"I ken what ye're thinking, lass," Ciaran said gently, reaching up to wipe a tear from her face. "And 'tis why I need tae do what I must tae clear my name, no matter how great the risk. 'Tis the only way we can be together."

"What if we left Scotland?" Isabelle asked, her desperation increasing. "Start a life somewhere new. I could still keep searching for Fiona, and you can keep thinking of ways to clear—"

"No," he said firmly. "I'll not take the coward's path and live a life on the run. My brother will never stop hunting me. And if we flee, he'll go after Gabhran, Lachaid, their families. I must end this. Isabelle," he continued, his voice softening, "I want ye tae be mine, to be my bride, to be at my side for always. I want tae give ye the life ye deserve. As lady of Aitharne Castle, wife of the laird. Not as the bride of an outlaw."

Isabelle bit her lip, divided. She wanted to be with Ciaran, more than anything. But not at the cost of his life. How could he not see how reckless his plan was, especially after what just happened with Walrick? There were so many things that could go wrong.

"I ken how foolish my plan seems—but I ken my brother. I didnae want tae see how dark he was, what he was capable of, but I do now. I ken how tae goad him, tae get him tae react and say what I need him tae say," Ciaran said.

"And if you fail?" Isabelle bit out. "If he captures you as soon as you set foot in that castle and has you killed?"

"Then ye return tae yer own time," Ciaran said without hesitation, and anguish filled her. "Ye go back tae yer life and ye live a long one. Ye find a man who—" his voice caught, and he seemed to force himself to continue, "who loves ye and will give ye the life ye deserve."

He left before she could protest further. Isabelle closed her eyes, blinking back tears.

It took several moments to calm down and pull herself from the haze of panic. When she finally did, she joined Ciaran and the others in the second drawing room. She hovered in the background, listening as they reviewed Ciaran's plan.

Ciaran planned to return to Aitharne Castle the next night, in the middle of the night to avoid detection. Ramsey and some trusted contacts would help them get into the castle and alert two other nobles they trusted.

Isabelle watched Gabhran and Lachaid closely as Ciaran spoke, hoping they would try to talk him out of it. Yet by the looks of resignation on their faces, she knew they'd agreed to his plan.

Isabelle took a shuddering deep breath. She'd just have to accept it as well.

As the meeting ended, and the men scattered, Ciaran approached her.

"I'm not going to try to change your mind," Isabelle said, at the look of wariness on his face. "But I'm coming with you tomorrow night."

"No," Ciaran said swiftly. "'Tis dangerous, and I'll not—"

"I'm coming," she repeated. "And if you put a guard on my door to stop me, I'll climb out the window and follow you anyway. Understood?"

She braced herself for more protests, but after a long stretch of silence, Ciaran smiled. He took her hand, lifting it to his lips in a kiss.

"I ken now not tae try tae sway yer mind, lass," he murmured. "Will ye dine with me alone tonight for supper? I've asked one of my men tae bring our meals tae my guest chamber."

Isabelle started to accept, but stopped herself. Was this some sort of last meal? A final stay before execution?

"As long as you promise it's not our last supper together," she whispered, her throat going dry.

"I cannae do that," he said, his eyes darkening with sadness. "But ye have my word I'll do everything I can tae ensure it isnae so."

WHEN ISABELLE CAME to his chamber for supper that evening, she let out a soft gasp. He'd taken care to make their meal romantic, setting up extra candles in the chamber. The soft illumination of the candlelight cast Ciaran in an almost ethereal glow; he looked even more handsome in his partially opened white tunic and red plaid kilt. His multicolored eyes filled with desire as they traveled over her body from head to toe. He crossed the room to her, taking her hands in his.

"I'm almost of a mind tae skip the meal altogether, lass," he said huskily. "In the candlelight, ye look like something out of a dream."

He kissed her, pulling her body close to his and probing her mouth with his tongue. Isabelle clung to him, not wanting to let him go, wishing she could prolong this moment.

But they reluctantly broke apart, sitting down to their simple meal of vegetable stew. They kept their conversation light; Ciaran seemed to go out of his way to avoid discussing his looming confrontation with Tavish. Instead, he asked her what her favorite books were, why she'd chosen to become a teacher, and for more details about the future. She giggled as his eyes went wide when she described hot showers in detail.

"And ye'd be willing tae give up such wonders tae stay in this time? With me?" he asked with a teasing smile.

Isabelle took his hand and leaned forward.

"Yes," she whispered. "All of it."

Warmth filled his expression, and he stood.

"Close yer eyes, lass," he murmured. "I want tae tell ye of another fantasy."

Intrigued, Isabelle did as he asked.

"Imagine . . . that we're wed and ye've just become my bride."

An explosion of joy filled her at the thought. She heard Ciaran move behind her, his large hands lowering to grip her shoulders. Her breath hitched as he reached down to lower the sleeves of her gown, revealing her shoulders. He gently kissed the exposed skin.

"We've returned tae our chamber after the festivities."

Isabelle held her breath as he tugged her to her

feet. She remained stock-still as he slowly stripped her of her gown, her tunic, and her underdress, until she stood naked before him.

"And we've hungered for each other all day," he whispered.

He turned her to face him. She wanted to open her eyes, but kept them dutifully shut as he peppered kisses from her throat to her chest.

"I've been hard for ye, and ye wet for me . . ."

Isabelle gasped as his mouth closed around one of her aching nipples, and his fingers dipped into her center.

"Ciaran," she whispered. "Please . . . can I open my eyes?"

"Not yet, my Isabelle," he returned. She yelped as he swung her up in his arms, and heat filled her when she realized that he must have disrobed as well; she could feel his naked flesh pressed against hers.

He lowered her to the bed, and she whimpered as he lowered himself to kiss her legs.

"And once I have ye in my bed, I begin tae devour ye," he growled. Isabelle clenched her fists, moaning as his lips moved up her legs to the juncture of her thighs. His tongue dipped into her center; he moaned. "And ye taste like heaven."

"Ciaran," she gasped, writhing beneath his mouth as her eyes flew open.

"Eyes closed," he said gently, nipping at her thigh, and she obliged with a moan of disappointment.

Sparks of pleasure rippled through her as Ciaran continued to feast on her until she could no longer hold off her release. As she cried out from the force of her orgasm, Ciaran kissed up the expanse of her abdomen, seizing each of her breasts in his mouth as he suckled her.

"Ciaran, please," she begged. "I want to see you."

"Then look at me, lass," he murmured. Her eyes flew open. He hovered above her, his hazel eyes infused with need. "Look at the man who loves ye . . . who would give his life for ye."

Her breath came out in a whoosh as he sank his hard length inside her. He began to move, and she wrapped her arms and legs around him, keeping her eyes locked with his, wanting to memorize every moment of his lovemaking, praying that this time wouldn't be their last.

CHAPTER 24

*A*itharne Castle loomed in the distance like a dark beacon. As Ciaran rode toward it, he realized he'd never seen it in the middle of the night from a distance. He could only vaguely make out its solid outline in the dark, as he was too far away to see the torches that lit the front gates. It was odd to return to his lifelong home as an outsider, with uncertainty and danger lying beyond its gates rather than the comfort he'd always known.

Ciaran turned to take in the men that rode with him—and Isabelle. It was the middle of the night; they had spent the day going over their plan of attack and ensuring their contacts in the castle could grant them safe passage inside without being caught. Isabelle had been quiet for most of the day; he'd hoped that their lovemaking and his hopes for their shared future would have calmed her. Instead, it only seemed to fill her with more anxiety.

She met his eyes. Though he could see the fear that lurked in their depths, and she clutched her reins so tightly that her knuckles were white, she gave him a wavering smile. He returned it, though his own fear swelled in his chest. His fear wasn't for himself; he'd come to a place of acceptance. His plan would either succeed and he'd defeat his brother, or it would fail, and Tavish would finally have him executed. It was as simple as that.

His fear was only for his Isabelle. He'd made Gabhran and Lachaid swear to get her to safety if his brother captured him; he'd also convinced them to leave him behind if their own safety became compromised. He'd not let his brother harm any of his men.

Ciaran returned his focus to the castle as they drew closer to it. Other than himself, Isabelle, Gabhran and Lachaid, ten men rode with them. The rest of the men rode yards behind them; they would remain out of sight beyond the castle grounds, approaching only if one of them signaled for help.

They rode up to the rear gates. Ciaran's heart picked up its pace as they waited. For several long moments he feared that their contacts had failed them. But to his relief, the gate soon lifted.

Ramsey stood there, along with Angus, and two guards still loyal to him. Ramsey gestured for Ciaran and the others to enter, and they did so, riding their horses through the empty and quiet courtyard to the stables.

"Tavish is awake and alone in his chamber," Ramsey whispered. "I did as ye asked—had a letter sent tae his chamber claiming tae have word of yer location. He's reading it now. Two other nobles are already in the adjoining chamber. Ye may not have much time with him, he may figure out what ye're trying tae do."

Ciaran gave him a sharp nod. He turned to face Isabelle, who stepped into his arms, wrapping her arms around his neck.

"You come back to me," she whispered, her eyes glistening with tears. "That's an order."

"Always," he said, leaning down to give her a brief but firm kiss.

He released her with reluctance. Gabhran and Lachaid both stepped forward to clamp their hands on his shoulder before leaving with Isabelle and the others. He watched them go; they were to hide in an empty guest chamber from which they could easily escape if things went awry.

Ramsey led Ciaran into the castle through the rear. It was silent and empty at this time of night; Ciaran could hear his footfalls echoing throughout the wide corridor as he walked. He trailed Ramsey up the winding stairs to the residential chambers. Nervous anticipation filled his chest as they made their way toward the chamber at the end of the hall, the chamber that had once been his.

"As soon as ye go in, I'll have the other nobles gather outside the door. Make certain tae leave it partially open so we can hear all that is said," Ramsey whispered.

They reached the chamber door, and Ciaran gave Ramsey a nod. Expelling a sharp breath, he pushed open the door and stepped inside.

Tavish stood in the center of his chamber, his eyes trained on the letter in his hands, using the illumination from the lit fireplace to read. He didn't look up at first, but when he did, he froze when he saw Ciaran. His eyes went from astonishment to fear to fury.

"GUARDS!" Tavish roared.

"I'm here tae turn myself in, but I only want a quick word alone with ye first," Ciaran said, holding up his hands in surrender, though he wanted nothing more than to strike his brother's murderous head with the hilt of his sword.

"I have nothing tae say tae a murderer," Tavish spat, clenching his hands into fists at his sides. "GUARDS—"

"What were our brother's last words?" Ciaran interrupted. Angus had managed to distract Tavish's guards for the time being, but they would soon return. He didn't have much time.

His words had their intended effect. Tavish blanched, his face going pale.

Good, Ciaran thought bitterly. *I hope ye feel some guilt in that dark heart of yers.*

"What?" Tavish faltered.

"Ye heard me. When ye killed him, what were his last—"

"I didnae kill Eoin," Tavish interrupted, though his eyes were filled with turmoil.

"Do ye hate me so much?" Ciaran pressed. He needed to keep pushing, to force Tavish from the avalanche of lies he'd buried himself beneath. "Tae murder yer own brother? Do ye not remember what our father said on his deathbed? That us three brothers were all we had. The only family."

A flare of emotion crossed Tavish's face, and Ciaran thought—hoped—he saw a flicker of guilt.

"Do ye want yer death tae be painful, brother?" Tavish hissed, his expression once again turning hard. "Keep talking and I'll make certain yer execution is—"

"'Tis yer jealousy that made ye set aside our father's words," Ciaran said. He took a breath, forcing himself to continue. He needed to push Tavish to the breaking point. "I've always been stronger than ye. A better leader than ye. 'Tis been that way from the start. Even had I not been the firstborn, our father would have preferred me."

Tavish stilled, his eyes going wild with rage.

"'Tis not true," Tavish spat. "Ye've had everything handed tae ye. Ye became laird only because ye were firstborn!"

"But I was even more respected as laird than ye," Ciaran taunted. "How do ye think I got intae the castle? That I've evaded capture for so long?

The servants are still loyal tae me—as are yer men. No matter how many ye kill or destroy tae get tae me, it will never change yer inferiority."

"A true leader does what is best for his clan!" Tavish roared. "Eoin was weak and ye focused only on yer power. I was the best one tae lead, but always ignored. With ye out of the way, Eoin would have been next in line tae lead. If I hadnae killed him, the clan would've faltered with his leadership. Eoin didnae even fight back. He just pleaded for me tae spare his life. And ye ran away—even confessed tae a murder ye didnae commit instead of fighting back! I'm the best leader for this clan, the best laird of this castle. And I did what it took tae prove it!"

Hot rage seared Ciaran's chest. He should have felt triumph; this was the confession he'd hoped for. But he could only see Eoin in his mind's eye, pleading with Tavish to spare his life before he was cruelly cut down.

With a ferocious roar, Ciaran reached for his sword and charged at Tavish, just as the door swung open behind them. Ramsey and several other clan nobles rushed into the chamber, followed by Gabhran, Lachaid, Isabelle and the others.

But Ciaran had reached his brother, pressing his sword to the center of his chest. Tavish stilled, his eyes flying past him to the other nobles in the room.

"Ye—ye planned this!" Tavish snarled. "Ye treacherous—"

"That word—and a great many others—refer tae ye," Ciaran hissed. He lifted the blade of his sword to Tavish's neck. All he had to do was sink the blade into his throat and watch him bleed out.

"Ciaran!" Lachaid shouted from behind him. "I ken ye want tae, and ye have great reason. But ye doonae need tae kill him. We all heard his confession."

But Ciaran was unable to move, his blade still pressed to Tavish's throat. Tavish had gone still now, his eyes trained on Ciaran's. Tavish's words kept circling throughout Ciaran's mind. *He pleaded for me tae spare his life.* Tavish deserved death for what he'd done.

"He begged," Tavish whispered. "The brother ye loved and swore tae protect, he begged me tae spare—"

"Ciaran!" Gabhran shouted. "He kens he's trapped and wants ye tae kill him. Doonae give him what he wants!"

"Ciaran."

Ciaran froze. It was Isabelle's voice. He heard her soft footfalls cross the room toward him. Tavish's eyes darkened at the sight of her; he must have recognized her as the lass who'd pretended to be a wayward traveler at Gabhran's manor.

Ciaran didn't take his eyes off of Tavish as Isabelle pressed her hand to his arm.

"You're no murderer. You're not Tavish," she whispered. "Think of our future. You won't be able to live your life with a clear conscience if you do this."

Ciaran swallowed, his eyes burning into Tavish's. She was right. He'd always known, even during his dark days in the dungeon, that he'd never be able to kill his own brother, no matter how much he deserved it. Even Eoin, in his infinite kindness, wouldn't have wanted Ciaran to murder Tavish on his behalf. And wouldn't it be a far better punishment for Tavish to live out his days imprisoned, far from the power he'd always wanted for himself?

He lowered his sword. Isabelle gently pulled him back from Tavish as Gabhran and Lachaid approached, taking Tavish by both of his arms.

"Take him to the dungeons," Ciaran said. "And call an emergency meeting with the other nobles."

Gabhran and Lachaid obliged, leading a pale and shaking Tavish out of the chamber. Isabelle's relief was palpable; she squeezed his hand as his nobles approached.

Ciaran closed his eyes, taking several shuddering breaths. Rage and despair still simmered within him, but from their ashes, a sliver of hope began to grow, like the seedling of a plant after a fierce storm. He had Isabelle at his side, and he'd returned home.

Think of our future, Isabelle had said. A bright one was possible; one that Eoin would have wanted for him.

"My laird," said one of his nobles, a man by the name of Graham, giving him a respectful bow when he opened his eyes. "Ye've been greatly wronged—and missed. We hope tae gain yer forgiveness. Welcome home."

CHAPTER 25

The next few days after the confrontation with Tavish seemed to fly by. Ciaran had Isabelle settled into her own private chamber adjacent to his, telling her he would move her into his own after they were wed. Her chamber was ridiculously large, more than double the size of her own apartment back in Chicago, complete with her own chambermaids. Her maids studied her with open curiosity and marveled at her strange manner of speaking. But they treated her with respect and kindness—she suspected they were just happy to have their laird returned to them, even if he'd returned with a lass who spoke with an odd tongue.

Ciaran had many matters to attend to after the nobles restored his titles. Tavish and the men he'd conspired with to frame Ciaran, including Walrick, were imprisoned or exiled. Tavish himself was confined to a life of imprisonment in the dungeons of an old crumbling castle that had belonged to an uncle of theirs on distant Aitharne lands.

After Tavish and his conspirators were dealt with, Ciaran brought Isabelle before the nobles and informed them that they were to wed. Isabelle braced herself, waiting for the barrage of protests, but there were none. Like his servants, the nobles loyal to him seemed so relieved to have him back they would have accepted any woman as his choice of bride.

"Ye have our congratulations," Ramsey said, giving Isabelle a nod. "Welcome tae Clan Aitharne, Isabelle."

Joy filled Isabelle's heart at the welcome, at the thought of starting her life with Ciaran.

But a shadow loomed.

It was the matter of Fiona and her absolute lack of progress in finding her. As soon as they settled into the castle, she and Ciaran sent several messengers to all corners of the Highlands for any word or rumors of lady Sassenachs with strange tongues such as hers. When a week went by with no word, the shadow turned into a dark cloud, one she knew would persist. How could she ever truly be happy until she was certain of Fiona's safety?

But her melancholy didn't persist for long. After a fortnight, one of the messengers returned with news. He'd learned that two lairds of a northern clan, Clan Macleay, had married Sassenach brides. Brides rumored to speak with odd accents.

"Their names?" Isabelle asked the messenger, her heart thundering.

And the names he told her nearly caused her to sink to her knees with hope and relief. Fiona . . . and Kara. The other missing woman.

Isabelle gave the startled messenger a hug before racing to Ciaran's study. He was deep in discussion with Lachaid, but at the sight of Isabelle, he dismissed him.

"What is it, lass?"

"Your messenger found her," Isabelle whispered, her eyes filling with tears. "He's found Fiona."

∼

MACLEAY CASTLE WAS QUITE a ways north from Aitharne Castle. They sent a letter north alerting the laird to Isabelle's visit. Ciaran insisted on having her travel by carriage and accompanying her.

"It's not necessary for you to come with me," she said. "I know you have much to tend to with the clan and your—"

"My mistake before was putting matters of the clan above the people I loved," Ciaran gently interrupted. "This is important tae ye, lass. I'm coming with ye."

They left just after dawn the morning after sending their letter to Macleay Castle, and Isabelle had to clench her shaking hands in her lap during much of the journey north. Could this Sassenach bride of Eadan Macleay be her Fiona? And what would she do if she wasn't? She pushed away the dark thought, choosing to cling to her hope instead.

When they arrived at Macleay Castle—a proud gray stone castle with several turreted towers—a servant greeted them in the bustling courtyard and led them into the great hall.

Isabelle froze when she saw the two people who stood waiting for them. A tall and handsome, dark-haired man stood next to . . . Fiona.

For a moment Isabelle couldn't breathe, not quite believing that the noble woman who stood before her in an emerald green gown was her Fiona. But the chestnut brown hair and warm brown eyes were the same, eyes that filled with tears at the sight of her.

"Izzy?" Fiona whispered.

Isabelle let out a strangled sob, and they both rushed forward, wrapping their arms around each other in a fierce embrace.

"I'm sorry I made you worry," Fiona said. "It was the last thing I ever wanted to do."

It was later that day. Isabelle and Fiona walked around the castle grounds, their arms linked. Ciaran and Eadan had left them alone to reconnect, and Fiona had promptly offered to give Isabelle a tour of Macleay Castle, her new home of the past few months. She'd told her everything that happened since she disappeared—arriving in the cellar of Macleay Castle, falling in love with Eadan, helping him deal with the attacks of another clan. She told her about the other traveler she'd met, Kara Forrester, now happily married to Eadan's cousin Ronan; they lived in a manor house not far from the castle.

When Isabelle told Fiona her own story of traveling through time and meeting Ciaran, she listened intently. She shook her head in amazement when Isabelle spoke of Kensa.

"She has to be the same woman I saw in Aberdeen. I suspected she was following me."

"She must have been," Isabelle agreed. "Right before I arrived here, she told me that neither of us belonged in the present."

"She was right," Fiona said. "This is where I belong."

Her hand drifted down to her abdomen, and Isabelle's eyes widened.

"Fiona . . . " she breathed. "Are you . . . ?"

"I'm pregnant," Fiona confirmed, with a wide smile. "It's early days yet, but I can tell."

"Oh, Fiona," Isabelle whispered, pulling her close. She'd only briefly seen Fiona and Eadan interact before he'd left them alone, but she could tell they were deeply in love.

"Eadan was worried at first. He almost insisted I go back to the present to have the baby, but I refused. He's having the best midwives sent from

Inverness and Edinburgh to assist with the birth. I'll be in good hands."

"Congratulations," Isabelle said, beaming. "I can't believe I'm going to be an aunt."

"You sure are," Fiona said. "I hope this means you're staying? Are you and Ciaran . . ."

"I love him," Isabelle said simply. "When I was back in my time, there was a heaviness in my heart without him. I came back not just to find you . . . but for him."

"I knew it," Fiona said with a grin. "He was looking at you as if you were the only woman in the world. Am I invited to the wedding?"

"Of course," Isabelle said, squeezing her hand. "You'd better be there."

She and Fiona spent the rest of the day commiserating. Fiona filled her in on details of her daily life at the castle, the time she spent with Eadan, what she did and didn't miss from their own time. Isabelle told Fiona about her future plans here; she had Ciaran's blessing to teach the children of the castle workers—and in the local village —how to read.

"I can see making a life here," she said, eagerness filling her at the thought of teaching again.

When Isabelle spoke of missing Scott, they discussed the possibility of her attempting to visit him in the future, or at the very least sending him letters as Fiona had done with her.

But those were concerns for another time, and she focused on enjoying her time with Fiona. They remained together until evening fell, and Ciaran fetched her to leave.

She embraced Fiona for a long time before leaving, and they swore to visit each other as often as possible.

As their carriage clattered away from the castle, Isabelle twisted in her seat to watch Fiona and Eadan disappear behind them, their arms around each other, their hands lifted in farewell.

A sense of calm settled over Isabelle. She had located her friend; she was happy, safe, and in love.

"Are ye happy?" Ciaran asked, when she turned back around.

"Happier than I ever thought possible."

"Good," he murmured, taking her hand. "Will ye marry me, Isabelle? Will ye be mine for always?"

Isabelle stared at him with a puzzled smile.

"I've already agreed to be your wife."

"It wouldnae have felt right getting wed with the uncertainty of yer friend's whereabouts looming. Now that ye ken where she is and that she's happy . . . ye can move forward."

Isabelle reached up to touch the side of Ciaran's handsome face, her heart swelling. Was it possible to love this man even more than she already did?

"You're right," she said, joy coursing through her. "And my answer is yes, Ciaran. I'll be your wife. With an open and clear heart. For the rest of my days."

CHAPTER 26

Present Day
Edinburgh, Scotland

Niall awoke with a gasp.

He'd just had the same dream that had plagued him for the past few months. In the dream, a beautiful woman with wavy auburn hair and sparkling green eyes approached him with a wide smile. She wore a high-waisted, long-sleeved, crimson gown, the type of gown worn by noble-women of the fourteenth century. An inexplicable joy had filled him as she approached, joy that melded with an odd sense of dread.

Niall expelled a breath, raking his hand through his hair. There were several varieties of this dream. In some, the woman looked morose, in others she looked terrified. And in others, her face was flushed with desire.

He'd tried to ignore the persistent dreams,

chocking them up to an overactive imagination or his lack of romantic partners as of late, but still they came to him.

He climbed out of bed, padding out of his bedroom to make his way to the kitchen of his spacious penthouse. As he made himself a kettle of tea, he tried to rationalize the recurrence of the dream. He was a historian; a researcher who consulted with museums and libraries over rare books and collections from medieval times. He came from an impressive pedigree of Scottish historians; his father before him had been an acclaimed historian, as had his grandfather.

Maybe he was having the dreams because of his latest consulting work with the Museum of Scotland over an exhibit about the lives of women in medieval Scotland. Or maybe he was still thinking about his friend Scott, a professor at the University of Edinburgh, who recently kept asking him for details about life in the Scottish Highlands in the fourteenth century—and wouldn't tell him the reason for his sudden interest.

But deep down he knew that neither of these reasons were the cause. He'd been having the dreams since before the consulting gig with the museum, and since before Scott started bombarding his email address with historical questions. He suspected the dreams were about something else. Something his family had been linked to for years.

Niall's family had the ability—though he would

personally call it a curse—to travel through time. His father had traveled so often that it had taken a toll on his health and killed him in the end. Other family members died trying to alter the course of history, while still others never returned from their travels and simply disappeared.

But Niall was determined that he would not become one of these wayward travelers, obsessed with the past. He had always been determined to stay fixedly in the present, to carry out his historical research through honest means—unlike his unscrupulous father. He'd never traveled through time, nor had the desire to . . . until the mysterious dreams.

He suspected the woman from his dreams was real, and that it was no coincidence she wore four-teenth-century clothing.

Niall poured himself a cup of tea, moving over to his large bay window. It was a bustling Saturday night and people were heading out to the pubs. He watched all the marvels of the twenty-first century —people on their cell phones, cars, and cabs clog-ging the streets, streetlights; he even spotted a distant plane flying overhead. Despite his profes-sion, he bore no nostalgia for the past. He'd never understood his father's—and other family members'—constant need to return to the dangerous and dark past.

But the recurrent dreams would force his hand, continuing until he sought out the mysterious woman.

Niall turned away from the bustling street, a weary sense of resolve settling in. He knew in his gut that he would have to return to the past, to find out who this woman was . . . and why she seemed to call out for him in his dreams.

Buy Niall's Bride (Highlander Fate Book 4) now. Keep reading for a brief excerpt.

When the world righted itself around him again, Niall found himself hunched over and clutching his knees on the ground, gasping for breath.

High-speed rollercoaster? He felt like he'd just fallen out of a plane and plummeted to the earth in free fall. Nausea twisted his stomach, and he took several deep breaths before stumbling to his feet.

He stood on the edge of the grounds of a sprawling stone castle, its front gates lit by torches. Some event was taking place; carriages and horses streamed in through its open gates.

He froze. *Horses and carriages.* There'd been a part of him that feared he'd still find himself in present-day Scotland. But as he took in the horses, carriages, and medieval clothing of the people he could make out from this distance, he realized that he was indeed in the past.

But what year? He squinted at the riders and the carriages. By the style of clothing and the carriages, he estimated late fourteenth or early fifteenth century.

"My laird? What are ye doing out here?"

Niall whirled to find a man standing behind him, his eyebrows knitted together in a confused frown. He looked to be in his early twenties, with warm brown eyes and dark hair. He wore a dark tunic and belted plaid kilt—well, what was the precursor to the kilt, though it looked close enough. Niall instantly recognized the distinctive Scottish brogue. He'd recognize the Highland accent anywhere, even one that differed slightly from the modern one. A sense of relief filled him. By the man's clothing and accent, he knew he was in the Scottish Highlands. He'd just have to make his accent match the others around him as best he could.

"My laird?" the man repeated. "How did ye get out here? And why did ye change yer clothes? Ye're the guest of honor."

Niall stilled, his heart thundering in his chest. Of all the scenarios he'd envisioned, this hadn't been one of them. His mind raced as he thought about what to do until he recalled something his father once told him about time travel.

"When all else fails, son," Ian O'Kean had said, his eyes twinkling. "Improvise."

"I lost my way," Niall said, hoping that he pulled off the accent. "And—these clothes suited me better."

The man stiffened, his eyes raking over him

from head to toe. *Did I pull it off?* Niall wondered with panic. *Or can he tell I'm an intruder?*

But the man gave him a brief nod.

"The guests are arriving . . . the feast will start soon," the man said, turning to head toward the castle.

Niall assumed he was supposed to follow, and trailed after the man, taking deep breaths to quell his panic. The man led him past the gates, through a bustling courtyard and past the grand double doors of the castle.

The historian in Niall wanted to stop in his tracks and gawk. He'd been in many castles all over Scotland and England, but in his time, most were decrepit ruins of what they'd once been. This castle was vibrant and full of life. Candlelight and torches lit the interior, dominated by high-arched ceilings and stone floors; the pungent scent of roasting meats and vegetables wafted into the large corridor from the kitchens, which was abuzz with the conversations of the many guests who made their way toward the great hall.

He had to force himself to keep following the man, to school his expression to one of neutrality, as the man led him into the great hall.

"There she is," the man said, with a smile that was almost teasing, gesturing at the head table. "Yer betrothed."

My betrothed? Fear tore through him as he followed the man's gaze, and his heart plummeted in his chest.

It was *her*. The woman he'd been dreaming of. And she was even more beautiful in person.

Long auburn waves framed her heart-shaped face. She had deep-set green eyes, delicate, feminine features, and she wore a gown of emerald green that enhanced the color of her eyes. He could detect the luscious swell of her breasts beneath the bodice of her gown, and he swallowed, his desire stirring like a sleeping dragon coming awake.

She was absently sipping a cup of ale, her gaze trained on the table before her, but she stiffened, as if sensing his eyes on her. Her eyes locked with his, and a faint, lovely flush spread across her cheeks. Arousal spread through Niall at the sight, and his mouth went dry. She was the loveliest woman he'd ever seen.

ABOUT THE AUTHOR

Stella Knight writes time travel romance and historical romance novels. She enjoys transporting readers to different times and places with vivid, nuanced heroes and heroines.

She resides in sunny southern California with her own swoon-worthy hero and her collection of too many books and board games. She's been writing for as long as she can remember, and when not writing, she can be found traveling to new locales, diving into a new book, or watching her favorite film or documentary. She loves romance, history, mystery, and adventure, all of which you'll find in her books.

Stay in touch!
stellaknightbooks.com

www.ingramcontent.com/pod-product-compliance
Lightning Source LLC
Chambersburg PA
CBHW030740110726
47900CB00008B/2382